GIFT OF

John Warren Stewig

Carthage

Kid Curry's Last Ride

A RICHARD JACKSON BOOK

Kid Curry's LAST RIDE

BY WARWICK DOWNING

ORCHARD BOOKS   NEW YORK

A DIVISION OF FRANKLIN WATTS, INC.

Orchard Books
387 Park Avenue South
New York, New York 10016

Orchard Books Canada
20 Torbay Road
Markham, Ontario 23P 1G6

Orchard Books is a division of Franklin Watts, Inc.

Manufactured in the United States of America
Book design by Mina Greenstein
The text of this book is set in 12 pt. Fournier
10 9 8 7 6 5 4 3 2 1

Library of Congress Cataloging-in-Publication Data
Downing, Warwick, 1931–
Kid Curry's last ride / Warwick Downing.
p. cm. "A Richard Jackson book."
Summary: Spending a summer in the 1930s with his grandmother in a
small Wyoming town, Alex becomes involved with an old man who
claims to be Kid Curry, a member of Butch Cassidy's gang.
ISBN 0-531-05802-6. ISBN 0-531-08402-7 (lib. bdg.)
[1. West (U.S.)—Fiction.] I. Title. PZ7.D7595Ki 1989
[Fic]—dc19 88-19822
CIP AC

TO JULIE,
for her art

$4,000.00 REWARD

DEAD OR ALIVE

Age: 37 years (1902)
Nativity: Dodson, Mo.
Occupation: Cowboy,
  train robber, horse and
  cattle thief, holdup man
  and murderer
Eyes: Dark
Height: 5 ft. 7½ inches
Weight: 145 to 160 pounds
Color: White
Build: Medium
Marks: Gunshot wound on right
  wrist. Slightly bowlegged
Personality: Reserved manner
  Drinks heavy, and has bad habits

HARVEY LOGAN alias

KID CURRY

Record: Killed Pike Landusky, of Landusky, Montana, Dec. 25, 1894. Robbed the Belle Bourche Bank, S. D., June 27, 1897. Escaped from the Deadwood, S. D. jail, Oct. 31, 1897. June 2, 1899, held up the Union Pacific at Wilcox, Wyoming. June 5, 1899, shot and killed Sheriff Hagen, Conners County, Wyoming. May 16, 1900 killed Sheriff John Tyler of Moab County, Utah, and Deputy Sam Jenkins. June 1900, killed the Norman Brothers. July 26, 1901 killed James Winter. July, 1901, killed Sheriff Scarborragh, Apache County, Arizona. March 27, 1901, killed Oliver Thornton, of Painted Rock, Texas. Dec. 13, 1901 wounded three deputies at Knoxville, Tenn. Captured, but escaped. June 7, 1904, held up the Denver and Rio Grande Railroad at Parachute, Colorado.

NOTIFY AUTHORITIES

Kid Curry's Last Ride

ONE

It was eight o'clock in the morning and summer vacation had started. I shouldn't even have been out of bed. But there I was in my dad's big old Packard, headed for the bus station. I sure didn't want to leave all my friends in Denver! But he was shipping me off to Sheridan, Wyoming, and I felt like a convict walking the last mile.

We rode down Fourteenth Avenue, which is paved all the way from Monaco Parkway into town. Big leafy trees hung over the street and made driving along it like riding through a tunnel, until we reached downtown where there aren't any trees. That's where all the streets are paved and there are so many cars and people you need traffic lights. New buildings stand around like giants, one or two of them as tall as ten stories.

I heaved a big sigh. Downtown is where the movie houses are, too, like the Paramount Theatre, which is easy to sneak into, and the Welton, and the Denham.

My dad parked the car on Tremont Street, and we pulled my suitcase out and went into the terminal to get my ticket. The bus wasn't there yet. "Well, where is it?" Dad wanted to know, glaring down at the dumb little ticket agent.

"I don't know, sir," the man said. He wore a bow tie and a white shirt and had garters on his arms to keep the cuffs from dragging on the counter. "The road up from Colorado Springs ain't paved all the way, sir, and it's terrible rough in places, and that's a fact. Maybe it had a flat tire."

"Well, did it leave Colorado Springs on time?"

"Oh yes, sir," the man said, looking up at my dad. "Yes sir, right on time. No doubt about it." He swallowed when he said it though, which bounced his Adam's apple around, which made his bow tie flutter around too, like a big moth, and I wondered if he really knew.

We bought my ticket and went outside and waited with the rest of the passengers for the bus to come. A boy my size, with one of those floppy hats that golfers wear, asked if we wanted a paper, and my father flipped him a nickel, even though he gets the paper delivered at home. "I don't understand it," he said, glowering at the headlines like they made him mad. "How the blazes did that man get elected to be president!"

"What?" I asked.

"Roosevelt! *I* didn't vote for him!" he declared, staring at the front page as if none of it made any sense. "Only an idiot would vote for him!"

I guessed there must be a lot of idiots then, because Roosevelt had been elected by a landslide. But I didn't say anything because I didn't want to get killed. "Bloody fool will get us into a war," Dad said. Then he jammed the paper under his arm and looked at his watch.

I hate it when he starts looking at his watch. It means he wishes he was someplace else. He and my stepmom were leaving Denver later on the same day—only they weren't going to a dumb old place like Sheridan. They were taking a train to New York City, where they'd spend a couple of days, then sail on an ocean liner to Paris, France.

He looked at his watch again and grumbled, and I knew what was next. When he doesn't have anything better to do, he gives orders. "Now I want you to be a good boy instead of a hellion this summer, young man," he said. I looked away, kind of hoping nobody else could hear him talking. "Are you listening to me, Alex?"

"Yes sir," I said. I was listening, all right. It's hard *not* to listen to my dad. He's a lawyer, and his voice is loud, and just then you'd have thought he was in court.

"Your grandmother doesn't get to see you that much," he went on, talking to me like I was the jury. "And as you know, you are all she has, after—well. You know what I mean."

He meant after my real mom died, but I was glad

he didn't explain that to everybody in downtown Denver. "Grandma got to see me all last summer, sir," I said, thinking that should have been enough to satisfy her. I'd been shipped off to Sheridan last summer too, when my dad and step-mom went to San Francisco and Hawaii.

"Yes, but remember, Alex, you're her only grandchild. And you look just like your mother did. And when she wants you to wear knickers, then you wear knickers," he said, looking at his watch again. "No ifs, ands, or buts. Do you understand me?"

"Yes sir," I said, thinking about how bad knickers itch.

Finally, the bus pulled up, which was a relief. We shook hands. "Now you be good," Dad ordered, looming over me and blocking out the sun.

"Yes sir."

Then he was gone. I was glad, I guess, but it left me with a lump in my throat.

That old Greyhound bus wasn't crowded at all. Who wants to go to Sheridan, Wyoming, if they can stay in Denver? I took a seat near the back, where I could sit by myself and look out the window. There wasn't much to look at once we'd left town and were headed north for Cheyenne. The telephone poles slid by like soldiers at attention, and I let my eyes glide along the wires that drooped in between. Every now and then a dirt road would come into the highway, and a car might be on it, dragging a big old cloud of dust behind.

Sheridan, Wyoming, I thought, watching some antelope chase around on the prairie. It was all right if you liked to hunt or fish or ride horses, but all my friends were in Denver, and besides, the dinky town was so small it only had one picture show. I tried to take a nap so I wouldn't have to think about it, but I couldn't even fall asleep.

Later, though, at night, it got to be peaceful and nice. The moon was so bright you could see the Laramie Mountains way off in the distance, with miles of prairie grass in between. The North Platte River ran alongside the road, and it was flat and wide and black as ink. When the angle was just right, the moonlight would skitter over the ripples like a silver shadow. A couple of times we caught a herd of antelope grazing near the road, and the bus set them off. A whole flock of silver-white rumps went bobbing and zig-zagging away, all like one thing, like birds changing direction in the sky.

Then all of a sudden, the driver was shaking me awake. "Hey boy, this here's Sheridan," he said, grabbing my suitcase and starting down the aisle. I stumbled after him, rubbing my eyes. It was light outside but the sun hadn't come up. "You got folks in this town?" he asked, setting my bag on the sidewalk in front of the Blue Bird Cafe, which was also the bus station. I nodded. "You be all right?" he asked anyway.

"Yes sir."

"Here. Put your coat on," he said, handing it to me.

"Ain't nobody here to meet you, boy. You sure you got folks in this town?"

"Yes sir, I'm sure."

"Well, let's get to a telephone and call them up."

"Oh, no sir, it's my grandmother. I don't want to wake her up. She'd kill me."

"She'd kill you, would she?" He looked up and down the empty street. "That big man back there in Denver, the one who put you on the bus . . . ?"

"Yes sir."

"He was a policeman wasn't he, boy."

"What? No. He's my father."

"Your father? You sure don't look much like him."

"No sir."

"You sure he wasn't a policeman, puttin' you on a bus to get you out of town?"

"No sir, he's my father. He's a lawyer."

"You sure you wasn't in some kind of trouble with the law?"

"No sir. I wasn't in any trouble."

"Well, all right then. I don't have to tell the sheriff you're in town then."

"Huh uh. Honest. I'm not a criminal."

"Well, I guess you don't look too much like a bad boy." He fished around in his pocket and pulled out a quarter and gave it to me. "Here."

"Gosh. Thanks."

"It's a tough life, kid," he said, climbing back on the

bus. "Don't get easier when you're older, neither." He cranked the handle that closed the door and nodded at me, then ground the bus into gear and drove off.

I picked up my suitcase and looked around. Nothing had changed in Sheridan. It all looked the same. The Five and Dime store was still across the street, and the laundry was still next to it. The Blue Bird Cafe didn't open until six, so I couldn't spend the quarter on a piece of pie. I looked through the venetian blinds to see what time it was, thinking maybe I'd wait—but it wasn't even five o'clock yet.

Maybe Jeff Pierce is up, I thought, remembering the friend I had from last summer. I decided to walk over to his house and see. I started down Main, which was the only paved street in town, and looked in the window at the Piggly Wiggly. Thinking about that pie had made me hungry, and I'd have liked to have got me a candy apple. But all I could see was cans and boxes of food, and that made me even hungrier.

The bank building looked just like it always had, and across the street from it was the old drugstore with a hitching post in front. That's where Jeff and I always went to get chocolate milk shakes and read comic books. I turned a corner, and just as I got to Jeff's house, the sun started over the hills east of town. Off to the south, you could see the Big Horn Mountains, blue and steep and cool. They rose up over Sheridan by more than a mile. There were big sheets of snow on the peaks and when the sunlight touched them, it turned them pink. I had to stop and look, it was so pretty.

It didn't look like Jeff was up—he wasn't outside, anyway—and his dad might hear me if I threw rocks at his window. So I went down two blocks to where my grandmother lived. I wanted to see the cave Jeff and me had dug in the vacant lot behind her house. Real quiet, I put my suitcase on Grandmother's porch, then went out in back to look.

I couldn't even find where it had been. It had been a big cave, too, with boards for a roof and bricks for a floor, almost tall enough to stand up in. There was some orange-looking dirt that didn't have any weeds growing in it yet. I guessed that was all that was left of our cave.

I was wide awake now, but I wasn't ready to see Grandmother Galdbreath. She wouldn't be up, and even if she was, it would be better to give her a chance for a cup of coffee. I remembered this old monkey cage at the Sheridan zoo, and felt like teasing the monkeys. I could chunk a couple of dirt clods at them and get them squawking. So I took off running for Kendrick Park, which is where the zoo was.

The park was stretched between Big Goose Creek on one side and a high, steep bluff on the other. You had to cross an old wooden bridge to get there. I found some flat rocks and when I got to the bridge, I tried skipping them on the water. But they wouldn't skip.

8

They just zunked in like hawks diving for trout. I cut across the grass for the monkey cage—about all there was to the Sheridan zoo.

The cage was butted up against the bluff, maybe fifty yards from the river. It had bars in front in kind of an arc, and inside the arc more bars and trapezes and all sorts of things for the monkeys to climb on. A cave had been dug into the bluff for them to sleep in at night, or get some shade if they wanted, and they could get in the cave through a small doorway.

But right away when I saw it, I knew something was wrong. A couple of bars were missing at the front, so if any monkeys had been in there they could get out. And the place didn't smell bad either, which was the way I remembered it.

Just then a hat came sailing through the door from the cave in back. I ducked behind a pine tree and peeked around. A man wearing coveralls and a blue shirt crawled through the door and went to stand up. He was bald on top but white hair hung down over his ears, and he was kind of fat. He stood up too fast and skinned his back against the top of the doorway. "Gol dang staggerack whumper!" he yelped—or that's what it sounded like. "Jehosophas! Judas Jehosophas!" He rubbed at his back. "Staggerack it anyways. Moby Dick!"

He found his hat—a Stetson, like the cowboys wear, but ragged and full of holes—and put it on. Then he climbed through the cage where the bars were missing.

9

"Humph!" He pulled a coin out of his pocket. "A nickel. A whole nickel. Kind of a breakfast will *that* get me?" He hitched up his pants and walked off. "Roosevelt's a liar. Don't like to call a man a liar but if he was to walk up to me right this minute I'd call him a liar to his face, and I don't care if he *is* the president. A whole country on welfare, but does that include me? It most staggerackingly whumper does not! Taxes. All them years . . ."

He wandered on down the road and kept right on talking, until his words blurred into each other like the sound of water in a stream. The last I saw though, his mood had changed. He was flipping the nickel in the air and trying to catch it behind his back, and I could hear him whistling.

My stomach started to growl again, right after he said "breakfast," so as soon as he was out of sight, I ran back over the bridge to Grandmother's house. I was hungry enough to eat a horse. I decided to wake her up and see if she'd fix me some pancakes.

Then I thought of the expression on the old man's face when he whacked his back in the doorway, and it made me laugh.

TWO

The next few days around that town were no fun at all. Jeff Pierce's voice had changed and he'd grown real big, his mom said, so they'd sent him to work on his uncle's ranch near Greybull. That meant I was on my own. There were two or three other boys I knew, but they were jerks. They belonged to a Boy Scout troop, and I couldn't see myself as a Boy Scout.

But my grandmother said she didn't feel sorry for me. I could walk up to Big Goose Creek any time I wanted, or hike over to Prairie Dog Creek and go fishing. The trouble with that was, I didn't know how to fish.

So I hung around the drugstore and read comic books, and even stole one or two. Or sometimes I'd sneak a quarter out of Grandmother's purse, then go to the movies. She didn't care. She played bridge most every afternoon, and when people were over, she'd rather I was off somewhere else.

It didn't take long to read all the comic books in the store and see the movie three times, and wish there was something else to do. If I was older I could be a cowboy and shoot Indians, or be like Pretty Boy Floyd that I kept hearing about on the radio, who robbed banks. . . .

It was in the morning when I thought of it. I was on Main Street, waiting for the drugstore to open, and the Sheridan National Bank was just sitting there across the street. It sure would be different to rob a bank.

Of course it wasn't much of a bank, compared to the ones I'd seen in Denver. The whole inside wasn't any bigger than a living room. And even though I didn't really mean it, I still got to wondering just how a twelve-year-old boy who was small for his age might go about it. Pretty Boy Floyd could just waltz in there with a machine gun, kill everybody in sight, and grab the money and run; but I wasn't even sure I could see over the counter. It was a problem, but maybe I'm like my dad in some ways, because I like working out problems. My mom used to tell me I might not look like him, but I was just as stubborn.

The drugstore hadn't opened yet so I shoved my hands in my pockets and wandered across the street for a better look. I peered through the big window near the door. Three men were already in there, working away. Two of them were in tellers' cages and the third one sat with his feet on a desk toward the back. The men in the cages had on white shirts and garters above their elbows and wore green visors on their foreheads. The man in the back was reading a newspaper. He wore tooled leather cowboy boots and was dressed as good as a movie star, with a coat and a string tie. He looked a lot younger than the others, and he wasn't really working either, so I figured he must be the boss.

I started to walk around the building, checking for windows or doors or anything I could see. Maybe there was some way to sneak in. The alley in the back was wide and full of weeds and grasshoppers, and two wagon ruts went down the middle, so I walked along it, pretending I wasn't even looking at the bank at all. Then I saw this door. No one was around so I hopped over there and looked for a doorknob. It didn't have one. It wasn't an ordinary door at all. It fitted into the wall as tight as a peg, which I learned when I tried to tuck my fingers in at the edges to see if I could pry it out. . . .

"You tryin' to get in the bank?"

I whirled around. The old man who lived in the monkey cage was standing there not more than ten feet away, and I hadn't even heard him come up. "What?"

"Just asked if you was tryin' to get in the bank. Seems to me, last time I looked, it had a front door. But here you are pullin' and tuggin' on that fire door, which don't have any handles on the outside and they keep it locked on the inside, and I was just curious."

"Oh. Well, see, I dropped a quarter out here yesterday and I thought, well, it might have got through the door."

He looked at me kind of funny. "A quarter? Get through that door? How would it do that?"

"Gosh, I don't know, guess I didn't really think about it."

He came over to the door and examined it himself. "That door's made out of steel. Don't see how a quarter could get through it, or even into the edges, it's built so tight. Was it open? Only time it's open is if there's a fire inside the bank. Was there a fire?"

"Well . . . could have been, I guess."

"I don't remember hearing the fire engine yesterday, or hearing anything about it. You sure?"

"Well, maybe just a fire in a wastebasket?"

"They ain't gonna open up that back door for no fire in a wastebasket! Not when all the money in town could get packed out of the very same door." He stuck a toothpick in his mouth. "Just don't see how a quarter could get inside. You certain that's what you was looking for?"

"Oh yes sir. It was right here that I lost it."

"You reckon maybe somebody stole it?"

"That must be it," I said, and I sure was relieved that there was a way to get everything explained. "Well, guess I'll be going."

"Wait a minute. You ain't gonna let somebody steal

a quarter off you and get away with it, are you? Ain't you gonna do something about it?"

He was watching me awful close. "Think I should get the sheriff?"

"Well a' *course.*" He grinned and kind of punched me in the arm. "Now that's what you should do, boy, when someone steals something from you—call the law. That's what *I'd* do. Hee hee!" He started off down the alley, laughing and talking to himself. "Call the sheriff! Well, Sheriff Buford ain't got anything better to do and he just might find the boy his quarter."

I couldn't tell if he believed me or not, but it didn't matter. He was gone, and I went back across the street to the drugstore. It had opened up, but I was having too much fun to go in and read comic books. I kept my eye on that old bank and kept pretending I was going to rob it.

Some people had gathered in front, talking and laughing, and then at ten o'clock the man with the suit opened the door. All the people on the sidewalk went in. None of them were in much of a hurry, like all they had to do that day was go to the bank, so after a while I wandered over too, like I didn't have much else to do either.

I pushed open the door and walked in. The place had a marble floor and spitoons by the tellers' cages, and behind the cages I could see the vault. I figured that's where they kept the money.

"What can I do for you, young squirt?" one of the tellers asked.

I had a dime and put it on the counter. I was tall enough to see over it easy. "Can I have some change please?"

"Two nickels, ten pennies, what?"

"A nickel and five pennies, please."

He counted it out and pushed it to me and I started to scoop the coins into my hand. "You're Dorothy Galdbreath's son, ain't you, who married that rich lawyer from Denver? Mildred Galdbreath's grandson?"

"Yes sir."

"Well, how's Dot? Now she's married to a fancy lawyer from Denver she don't ever come back to Sheridan. Wait, now didn't I see something in the paper about . . . Oh." He looked at me and frowned. "Well, I'm sorry about your ma, son. . . . Say, you been fishing yet?"

"No sir."

"You ain't been fishing! Well, what are you waiting for! The water's down and they're hungry, don't you know that? You better get out to the creek before Marv over there starts up. He'll catch 'em all."

"I don't have a fishing pole."

"Well, you got a pocket knife don't you?"

"Yes sir."

"That's all you need, and some string and a hook, and you can go out there on Big Goose and find a willow and cut yourself a pole. That's all there is to it."

"Need something better'n string," the other teller said. I guessed that was Marv. "Most fish close to town have got so they recognize string. They'll chew right through it." He was counting a stack of bills. "Course if you get far enough out of town, you can still use string. Them country fish are awful dumb. They don't go to school, you see." He looked around, like he was disappointed in something, and all the first teller did was shake his head. "Get it?" Marv asked me, kind of hopeful. "School? Fish?"

"Yes sir."

"Dang it, lost my count."

I put the change in my pocket and went outside. If I ever robbed that bank, I decided to shoot Marv. It would be more like putting him out of his misery. I walked across the street and got in the shade again, in front of the drugstore, but still couldn't come up with a plan.

Then a lumpy shadow stood up and turned into a person. It was that old man again! He came over by me and leaned on the two-by-four railing in front of the store. "Ain't you Mildred Galdbreath's grandson?" he asked.

"Yes sir."

"She sure is a pretty woman, considering her age. Don't see how she stays so pretty and thin."

I could have told him how she starved herself to death and practiced different expressions in front of the mirror.

"Then I guess your father is that rich lawyer from Denver, ain't he?"

"Guess so."

"Mmm." He spit into the street. "I been watching you, son. You seem almighty interested in that bank." *That* put a scare in me. How'd he know that? "How come you're watching that bank so close?"

"Who, me? The bank?"

"Humph," he said, then looked across the street at it. "Ever hear of Kid Curry?"

"No sir."

"He was an outlaw in these parts, rode with Butch Cassidy and the Wild Bunch, not all that long ago either. Made his living robbing banks. Most people think he got killed about thirty years back, over in Parachute, Colorado."

"Oh."

"He didn't, though. Know how I know?"

"No sir."

"Well, before I tell you, I got to find something out. Can you keep things to yourself or are you like an old woman of the kind who will blab everything she hears all over the town? Or even go to the law? In other words, boy, are you one of them there bigmouths who can't keep anything in, or not?"

Gosh. An outlaw? "I won't tell."

"I got your word on that?"

"Yes sir. You got my word."

"All right then." He leaned on the rail and stared into the street. His eyes leveled out. "Reason I know is because I'm Kid Curry myself, and I ain't dead yet. That posse in Parachute hung the wrong man." He shifted his weight to his other foot, and the railing creaked. "I been lookin' that bank over too, the one you been eye-ballin', and it's just a-settin' there waitin' for somebody to take it. Why, if a man had the right kind of partner, he could knock it over . . . " He snapped his fingers. "Just as easy as that."

THREE

It really surprised me what the old man said.

"You mean that bank across the street?"

"Reckon I do, son," he answered, still leaning on the hitching rail in front of the drugstore. "It's the only bank in town."

I cleared my throat. "Well, how would you do it, Mr. . . . ?"

"Call me 'Kid,' " he said, and spit again. "I'd just bust in there and hold it up, then get on a horse and ride like I was in front of a stampede. I'd head for the Big Horns—know those mountains like a woman knows her kitchen—and I'd pick a spot and hide out a week or two, then easy as pie, slip into Montana."

"What would you need a partner for?"

He gave me a patient look, like my father does when I ask him something stupid. "Somebody has to hold the horses. There ain't no time to waste when you leave a bank carrying a canvas bag full of money. I wouldn't want some near-sighted bank clerk to put a hole in me while I untied my mount from the hitching rail."

"Wouldn't you just kill all the clerks?"

"Kill all the clerks! Now ain't *you* the blood-thirsty one! They ain't robbin' *you*, boy. *You're* the one who is robbing *them*." He shook his head. "Kill all the clerks. I see where some education wouldn't hurt *you* none."

"What if somebody was to follow?"

"That's the beauty of it. They couldn't follow unless they was on horseback, because we'd go where there ain't roads. And most people live in town now, and most of 'em ain't even got a horse!" The rail groaned with his weight, and for a minute, I thought it might break. "As easy to rob that bank as walkin' upside down is to a spider."

"What?"

"I mean it might *look* hard, but it wouldn't be any trick at all to rob that bank. No trick at all."

He stood up and to tell the truth, I was glad. If that rail had broken he might have spilled out into the street and busted his neck. "What're you called?" he asked.

My real name is Alexander Penrose III, but I didn't want to tell him that. Even "Alex" isn't my idea of a name. When I look in the mirror and draw my cap pistol, I always call myself *Rico*, so I gave him that one. "Rico."

"Huh!" The skin between his eyebrows bunched up. "I knew a cowboy once, called himself 'Rico,' down in Nevada. Got caught palmin' cards, so they hung him." He turned his back to the rail and leaned against it, watching me. "That ain't your real name. What's your real name?"

"It's, uh, Alexander."

"Well, Alexander what? You got a last name, don't you?"

"Yes sir. Penrose. Penrose III."

"You don't say!" He laughed, just like I knew he would, kind of hard and mean. "Now that's more like it, for a rich lawyer's son. I suppose you'll want me to call you Your Highness, or the Duke of Penrose, or . . . "

"It isn't *my* fault what my name is!"

He looked at me and must have seen how something had gone wrong with my face. "Reckon not. *You* wouldn't 'a given yourself a name like that. That name don't fit you, either—you bein' a little feller, prob'ly tough as rawhide, kind of quiet, not like a lawyer's son at all." He put his elbows back down on the rail and it sagged toward the ground. "I know'd another cowboy, this one from Montana, didn't talk or laugh much but he was tough as barrel cactus. I seen him get into it one time with one of the biggest, loudest bullies in the whole state, wear that man down with sheer grit, then put him into a horse trough. Had to have help gettin' him into it because the bully was twice his size and that little feller couldn't no more

22

pick him up than he could pick up a building, but the bully didn't know the difference, not then." His hand bounced off the top of my head. "You sorter remind me of that cowboy. Know what they called him?"

"No sir."

"Now there is something you got to get over. A 'sir' is either an officer or a gentleman, and I ain't any such thing, and don't ever want to be confused with such things." He turned his head and spit again. "If we're gonna ride together, you got to call me by my name, and it's 'Kid.' "

"Okay. Kid."

"That's better." He grinned at me, and I thought he liked being called "Kid" again. "They called that cowboy 'Cloudy.' It fit with his usual expression, which wasn't exactly sunshine and blue sky. Even after puttin' that bully into the horse trough, he didn't allow himself to smile. Now you look about as tough as that cowboy, so I'm gonna call you Cloudy."

I grinned inside myself. It made me feel good. "That's okay."

"Tell you what, Cloudy, you think it over, what I been talking about. Course if you want to take that bank on by yourself, I won't stand in your way. You're a young man and young men like to do things for theirselves without any help. You might not even need a plan, just as an example. You might be a natural at robbin' banks, and go ahead and do it, then high-tail it out of town on a scooter or something, and you might even get all the way to the edge of town before they catch you and put you in jail.

"Robbers generally pull about twenty years of hard time, a' course, if they get caught, which is something you should keep in your mind when you consider the odds. But if you want some help with this thing and would like a partner with some experience at robbin' banks, well, you can come talk to me most any time you want. You know where I'm stayin'. The monkey cage at Kendrick Park.

"Now don't start in lookin' like you don't know what I'm talkin' about. I seen you peekin' around. . . . Matter of fact, I had a notion to ask you in for supper last Tuesday, but all I had was leftovers, you might say.

"So you think about it, Cloudy. Then drop by the monkey cage in a day or two and tell me what you've decided to do."

I didn't know how I'd ever let him know anything, because trying to get a word through to him was like trying to pour water through a rock. I started to tell him it sounded okay to me, but I was too late.

"Yes sir, I'll just wait on your decision, but there ain't no secret, exactly, about what I hope you'll decide. I'm a-hopin' maybe the two of us can be partners and get into the bank withdrawal business, which is how I used to make a living and I kind of miss the excitement of it, to tell you the truth." His eyes were as bright as if he'd found a hundred dollar bill in the street. Then he started waddling down the sidewalk and I almost called him back, because I was ready to get into the bank withdrawal business right away—but I got to thinking: Do I really want to rob a bank? Bank robbers get shot at and killed. What if some near-sighted clerk was to put a hole in me?

He sure could make it sound easy, though, and my father always told me how I should listen to my elders. Well, maybe I'll do what he said, I thought, and listen to this old man, and help him rob the Sheridan bank. Then if I get caught and the sheriff is hauling me to jail, I'll say when they're throwing away the key, "Dad, all I did was follow your advice."

But the more I thought about it, the more I wondered if that old man even was a dangerous outlaw. He sure didn't look dangerous to me. I decided right then and there that if I was going to rob a bank, I wanted to do it right, and not go off half-cocked with some old bum who'd get us caught.

Golly, though, I thought to myself, kind of glad my dad had sent me to Sheridan after all. What if he really *is* Kid Curry? It sure would be different to rob a bank with a famous outlaw!

FOUR

If Kid Curry was famous only thirty years ago, Grandmother Galdbreath would have heard about him. I'd go ask her. She'd lived in Sheridan all her life, and I didn't know how old she was exactly, but she was a lot more than thirty.

The trouble was when I got back to her house there were cars parked in front, which meant some of her friends had come over to play bridge. None of those old ladies needed a car. The town was so small they could walk to anywhere they wanted, but each of them had a car anyway.

"Why Alexander, what are you doing here?" Grandmother asked, trying to make it sound like she was glad to see me, even though she wasn't. "Come in, dear. Say hello."

"Hello."

"Do you need something, honey-bunch? I'll bet if

you look, you'll find a quarter in my purse. There's a new movie at the Fox."

"Saw it yesterday."

"Well, you're not just going to sit inside and mope, are you? It's such a beautiful day!"

"Heavens to Betsy, Mildred, let the boy be," Miss Landusky said. She was older than my grandmother, and her cheeks hung down to her belt, and the glasses she wore were as thick as your thumb. I kind of liked her, though. She'd seen me swipe a comic book at the drugstore the Saturday before, but had guessed I'd forgotten to buy it out of being "pre-occupied" or something. But she made sure I put it back. "How are you, Alexander?" she asked. "I expect you're bored to death."

"No ma'am. Not since . . ." But then I didn't know what to say. Not since I'd met a dangerous outlaw and was working on a plan to rob the bank?

"Since when?" Miss Landusky asked. She was frowning, and it looked like she couldn't make up her mind over which card to play.

"Well, I heard there was a famous outlaw in town," I said, forgetting all about my promise, and then re-membering it. "I mean, not in town *now*, but from around here."

"There certainly are a lot of outlaws in Sheridan, but not that many of them become famous," Miss Landusky said. "I can think of several, as a matter of fact."

"Really?" I asked.

"Lavonica is teasing you, dear," my grandmother said. "She thinks most of the good people in Sheridan are bad."

"Not bad, Mildred, just suspect. Goodness, I wish I could make up my mind!"

"We all do, Lavonica dear," one of the other ladies said.

"Well, what about Kid Curry?" I asked.

The question seemed to come as a real surprise. Miss Landusky even had trouble holding on to her cards.

"Alex, you may watch us if you must, but we *are* playing bridge and it *does* require concentration," my grandmother said. "Please, dear. No more questions."

"That's all right, Mildred," Miss Landusky said, and played a card. Her hands were shaking, though, and she kind of blushed. "I knew Kid Curry, Alexander." Everybody at that bridge table was still, and I wondered why things had gotten so strange.

"Is he an outlaw?"

"Perhaps more accurate to say that he *was*," Miss Landusky said. Then the lady whose turn it was got a gleam in her eye and put a card down on top of Miss Landusky's.

"Oh!" Miss Landusky said.

Grandmother gave me a look, so I started to leave.

"Just a moment, Alex," Miss Landusky said. "You know, I'd enjoy it very much if you were to come visit with me some afternoon. I was very fond of your mother and you remind me of her. I'd like to get to know you." I tried as hard as I could to look enthusiastic. "We could talk about Harvey—that is, Kid Curry—as well as other things, possibly, such as what you intend to do with your life."

"Alex would be delighted, Lavonica," my grandmother said.

I wasn't so sure. But I went over the next day, and I'm glad I did.

Miss Landusky lived in a big house on Coffeen Avenue. There were shade trees in front and lilac hedges around the sides, and a stone sidewalk that wandered from the street to the porch. She was rich as anything, Grandmother had said, so she wanted me to be nice for a change. She even dressed me up in knickers, which were tight and made out of wool, and it was hot and they itched like stinging nettle.

"Good heavens, Alex," Miss Landusky said when she saw me. "How can you stand wearing knickers on a day like today? And flowers! Goodness, boy. Mildred's idea?" She took the flowers out of my hand and smiled.

"Yes'm. No'm."

"*That* certainly covers the situation."

"I mean, the knickers weren't my idea, but the flowers were." I figured a little lie wouldn't hurt. "I picked 'em at Kendrick Park."

She laughed, and a lock of hair curled over her forehead. I wondered if a long time ago she'd been pretty. "I expect it was *all* Mildred's idea, but it's nice of you to pretend it wasn't." She took a vase off the mantel and stuffed the flowers in, then took one out and pinched off some of the stem and put it back in a different place. It only took a minute but when she was done, she'd turned them into something that looked real nice.

Then she gave me pie and ice cream—cherry pie, just a little sour, which was perfect—and watched me eat it. It only took two seconds. That seemed to make her feel good, so to make her feel better, I had another piece.

I didn't want to ask her about Kid Curry right away. "You sure have a lot of books," I said, noticing that one whole wall of the room we were in was covered with them.

"The accumulation of a lifetime, Alex. The nice part about books is that through them, I can go all the way back—even behind my own lifetime—clear to the dawn of history." She smiled. "Do you like to read?"

"No'm. I hate it."

She laughed again, kind of at herself, then moved in her chair so she could see me better. I wondered what she was thinking about. "I suspect it's still as different between boys and girls as it used to be. When I was your age, girls weren't expected to do much of anything except clean house and feed the men and chickens." She looked kind of disgusted about something, but I didn't know what. "I used to read a great deal when I was a girl. The boys never did, of course. The boys—in Montana at any rate, where I was raised—rode horseback and hunted, and wrangled cattle and fought Indians, and when they got a little older, every so often they'd shoot one another. *Much* more exciting to be a boy, but as a rule the girls lived longer."

"Yes'm."

Then she started in telling me what it had been like living in Montana in the 1880s and 1890s, and it was real interesting. I found out that the name of the town she'd been raised in was Landusky, after her people, and that it was in the Little Rockies, which was the name of some mountains up there, and that the town was so small that to her a place like Sheridan with four or five thousand people was still pretty big. "Of course it isn't as large as Boston, which is near where I went to college, but quite honestly Boston—and Denver—and New York—those cities are just too large. At least for me."

"You went to college?"

"Yes. My mother sent me there after . . . what happened . . . and I expect old Pike Landusky, my stepfather, is still spinning in his grave over the matter of my education. For anyone to go to college struck him as the height of foolishness, and for a female to go was downright sinful!"

"What was it that happened?"

"My stepfather was killed when I was sixteen. My mother sent me to Wellesley after that—a college for women, and quite a good school—and it ruined me, of course, because I discovered I can think as well as a man. Quite frankly, I'm glad for the ruination."

"Golly. You mean your stepfather got killed? How?"

"Old Pike was shot by a young man I'd been seeing. At the time, it seemed very tragic and—romantic." She took a deep breath. "How utterly foolish it seems to me now."

I didn't know what she was talking about, which happens all the time when grown-ups talk. But it sure gave me a different feeling about her. For one thing, she hadn't been a grown-up all her life. "What happened?"

"Oh, he deserved it, I suppose, if it's possible to deserve that sort of thing," she said, her voice low. "It was Christmas Day and the men had been drinking. Then Pike and my young man started after each other. Harvey Logan—my young man—didn't really want to fight, but of course it wasn't possible for him to back down." She smiled in kind of a funny way and rocked her head. "They'd been fighting with their fists—actually, I was the reason they were fighting— and Pike was getting the worst of it. He couldn't stand losing to someone he regarded as a boy—isn't it awful!—so he drew this brand new automatic pistol out of his belt, and aimed it at Harvey, and pulled the trigger."

She stopped, right when it was getting good, and shook her head again.

"My gosh. What happened, Miss Landusky?"

"Nothing. The pistol had a safety mechanism on, and Pike had never owned a pistol with a safety mechanism. But of course it frightened Harvey, and before anything further happened, Harvey found his pistol and shot at Pike. He killed him." She smiled, kind of sad.

"Wow."

"Later, Harvey joined a group of outlaws, and they called him 'Kid Curry.'"

"You mean your boyfriend was Kid Curry?"

She nodded, like it didn't mean anything to her now, but her hands shook, and I swallowed. That old man who lived in the monkey cage had been her boyfriend!

"I was very much in love with him, of course," she said. "I was certain we'd be married some day, but after shooting Pike, he had to run and . . . Well. Perhaps I should have run away with him, but I didn't."

It was easy to see how sad it made her, but she'd gotten over it, just like I finally got over the blues after my pony got hit by a streetcar. "He was far and away the handsomest man I'd ever known," she told me, "but he was also quiet and just as lonely as a tree growing alone on the prairie. I was quite a talker, however, and as a consequence, one could say we got along quite well together." She smiled—not at me— then let her head roll back and forth like she wondered about all kinds of things. "He was such a gentle man, too—with me, at any rate—and it has always been hard for me to believe those terrible things they say about him. Have you seen his poster?"

What she said about him being quiet made me wonder a little, because the Kid Curry I knew was a nonstop talker. "No'm. What kind of poster?"

"A wanted poster. He was a wanted man. Fair game." She pushed her way out of her chair and got over to a desk and opened a drawer. "Isn't it odd?" she asked, and I made the mistake of thinking she was talking to me.

"What?"

"Life," she said. "Let me show you his poster."

I hadn't any idea in the world what she was talking about, but it didn't matter. The poster was made out of heavy paper, and had a picture of a man with black hair and a mustache, and it said, "$4,000.00 Reward, Dead Or Alive."

"Gosh." I kept on reading. "Did he do all this other stuff too?" I read where he'd killed a couple of sheriffs and their deputies and escaped from jails and kind of wedged in robbing banks when he wasn't in a gunfight.

"So they say. Of course, all those people were hunting him, and when they shot his way, he would quite naturally shoot back. They wanted to put him in jail, and the very thought of jail—penned up in a cage like an animal in a zoo—the thought of it was worse than death to Harvey."

34

"But why did he run away after he shot Pike?" I asked. "If it wasn't even his fault, why didn't he stay and have a trial?"

She smiled at that. "Of course your father is a lawyer, and well you might wonder at that. But there weren't any lawyers in Landusky in 1894," she said. "There were a lot of Pike's kin, however, and if Harvey hadn't run away, they would have hanged him. That's just the way things were done then." She looked at me. "You see, there's been *some* improvement."

"Did you say he didn't like cages?" I asked, suddenly remembering something else about the old man. He was *living* in one.

"He thought cages were terrible! The last time I saw him—oh, dear," she said, blushing.

"You mean you saw him after he shot Pike, Miss Landusky?"

"Yes. Many, many years ago we met at the Brooklyn Zoo, of all places, and if I hadn't been there, he'd have opened up all the doors and let the animals out."

"Why would he do that?" I asked, but then I kind of laughed. "It sure would be a surprise." I started to give her the poster.

"You can keep that, if you'd like."

"I can? Gosh, thanks!"

"What is it you really want to know, Alex?"

"Oh. Nothin'." It kind of caught me off guard. "I just heard some men talk. Over by the bank."

"Goodness. You aren't thinking of robbing the bank, are you?"

"Oh, no'm." My gosh, I wondered. Why did she say that? Is she still thinking about that stupid comic book?

"I certainly hope not, because outlaws—in spite of all the glamor and glory—really don't do very well." Then she started in telling me about the gang of outlaws Kid Curry rode with when he wasn't off by himself.

They had been called The Wild Bunch, she said, because they were pretty wild. There was Butch Cassidy, who was the leader and smart as a whip; and Sundance, who was a ladies' man, but deadly as a snake; and a man they called "The Tall Texan," but she didn't know much about him. There was also Flat-Nose George, and Kid Curry, and the Kid's brother, Loney, and some others too. They robbed trains and banks all over Wyoming and the Dakota Territory and into Minnesota, and once in a while they'd drop into Colorado or go over to Utah, where Butch was from. Then after robbing a bank they'd run for a place called "Hole-in-the-Wall," which was about a hundred miles south of Sheridan but before you get to Casper. I had the feeling she'd known them pretty well, the way she talked, but I didn't ask. "Where are they now?"

"Dead. There're all dead, Alex. They hang outlaws when they catch them, or shoot them with bullets. And

36

that's what happened to all of those boys." She shrugged. "A pity."

"Kid Curry too?"

"Why do you keep asking about Kid Curry?"

"I heard somebody say they saw him in town," I said. "About a week ago."

Her hands wouldn't stay still. They reached out in the air for something that wasn't there, then plopped in her lap. "People have been seeing him for years, Alex."

"How could they, if he's dead?"

"Because no one is absolutely certain. The man they think was Kid Curry was hanged in Colorado, but the sheriff buried him rather too quickly. The reward was never paid."

"So he could still be alive?"

"It's possible, but it isn't very likely. He lived a violent life and I'm quite certain he died a violent death."

I dug out the poster. "Is that the way he looked?"

"I suppose. Thin face—beautiful black hair—eyes that could be very soft, or very cruel."

That old man in the monkey cage? "Would you recognize him if you saw him now?"

"He'd have put on a few pounds, but I'd recognize him. I wouldn't want to, though. He's still wanted for murder."

It felt like an oyster had crawled into my throat. "Really?"

"Is something wrong, Alex? Is there anything you'd like to tell me? I'm actually very good at keeping secrets."

"No'm, Miss Landusky, but I'd better be going. Thanks a lot."

"Must you leave so soon? We haven't even talked about you."

"Oh. Well . . ." I really wanted to get out of there.

"Never mind, we'll do that another time," she said, starting to stand up. "Perhaps if you don't wear knickers next time, you can stay longer." I'd forgotten about how they itched, and now they started up again.

"Incidentally, the sheriff has asked me to look at several men in the last few years who claimed they were Kid Curry. None of them were, of course."

"My gosh. Why would anybody want to say they were Kid Curry and get hung for murder? Especially if they aren't?"

"I don't know, Alex. Boys will be boys."

FIVE

I took off those knickers as soon as I could, and the temperature went down twenty degrees. Then I hid the poster Miss Landusky had given me under a corner of the rug in my room, and put on pants and got out of there before Grandmother even knew I'd been back.

Kid Curry was a dangerous outlaw all right. I even had a wanted poster to prove it, but there sure were a lot of questions in my mind. Was that old man in the monkey cage really Kid Curry? I ran all the way to Kendrick Park, hoping he'd be there so I could ask him some questions.

He was there. He was asleep under a tree, his hands laced over his stomach and a peaceful expression on his face. If he was a dangerous outlaw, I thought, wouldn't he be on his guard? How did he live to be an old man if a twelve-year-old boy could sneak up on him? I decided to throw a pine cone or two at him to wake him up, like I was a squirrel who wanted him to move. I got behind the tree and started to drop one on his head—

"Now don't do anything might get you into trouble with me, son," he said.

"What? Who? Me?" I asked, and saw his left eye was part of the way open and aimed at me.

"Just what do you plan to do with that there pine cone?"

"Oh. Well, I saw a mosquito on you and I was going to drop it on the mosquito."

"That ain't bad, Cloudy," he said, sitting up. "You had to come up with something quick, and that wasn't too bad. Mosquitoes don't bother me none though, son, so you can put down that pine cone and set. You see, I'm so mean I make them sick."

I sat down, but not too close. "Are you really Kid Curry?"

"Well, now let me see," he said, squeezing his arm. "Last time I checked myself, I was. Course I haven't asked the sheriff whether I am, because they're still looking for me and I don't want to go to no jail! I ain't ever been *that* hungry. But I reckon I know who I am, all right, and it's Kid Curry. Why do you ask?"

"I saw a 'Dead or Alive' poster, where they offer a reward—"

"You saw what? Where?" His legs kind of pulled up under him, like he was ready to take off out of there, if he had to. "Who you been talkin' to, boy? The law?"

"No sir, just an old woman. Miss Landusky."

"Lavonica? Does she know where I am?"

"No sir, I didn't tell her anything like that."

"Well, just what did you talk to her about then? And don't call me sir!"

I gulped. He kind of scared me. Besides, I was the one who wanted to ask *him* questions. "Just—about Montana a long time ago, and the Wild Bunch. But I didn't tell her anything."

He kind of relaxed, and his eyes got that far-away look, like Miss Landusky's had. "Sure been a heap of years since I saw Lavonica," he said.

At least he knew Miss Landusky's first name. "Did you know her pretty well?" I asked.

"You could say I knew her, all right. She was about the prettiest thing anywhere in the world. Smart, too, even went to college. Not worth a durn thing after that, of course. Started in worryin' about whether the Indians was being treated right, and such things as that."

"What about her stepfather? Did you know him too?"

"She tell you about how I shot old Pike?" he asked, glowering at me something fierce. "Durn woman. Did she tell you why?"

I nodded, still wondering if he was, or if he wasn't. "She told me how handsome you were, too, and how thin."

He started picking his teeth with a pine needle, then gave me a look. "Is that what this is all about, son?"

he asked me. "You been wonderin' whether or not I'm really the Kid?"

"You don't look much like the man on the poster," I said.

He nodded, like he finally understood what was going on. "I never *did* look much like that drawing on that danged poster," he said. "That picture was drawed by a chimpanzee whose arms had been cut off and had to work with his feet."

"It says you have black hair and are thin."

"I *did* have black hair twenty years ago, and I was thin, too. But about ten years ago, Cloudy, I don't know why, but one day my hair just up and turned white." His legs relaxed and he leaned his back into the tree. "About the same time I shrunk about a inch and gained thirty pounds. Dangdest thing. I used to never could sleep, either, which is why I was so thin maybe, always tense inside and waiting for something bad to happen. But ten years ago I just got so's I didn't care *what* happened, and now I sleep so good it takes an explosion to wake me up.

"Here." He dug a billfold out of his back pocket, so old it was falling apart, and pulled a photograph out of it. "Ever see her before?"

I stared at the picture, trying to remember where I'd seen one just like it. The woman it showed had a smooth round chin which she held high, and soft eyes, and a sad-happy mouth like my mother's. Then all of a sudden I remembered I'd seen one just like it that

42

afternoon, on the mantel at Miss Landusky's house. "Is that Miss Landusky?"

"That's right, Cloudy. She don't look much like that now, though, does she?"

"Huh uh," I said, agreeing with him. "She's really changed."

"That's what happens when you get old and gray."

"She also told me how quiet you are."

"Mmm." He took the photograph and kind of wrapped that old billfold around it. "Used to be when I was around people, I never had much to say. But I always talked a lot, off by myself. Now it just don't seem to matter whether people are there or not." He got the billfold back into his pocket, where it was safe. "My talking bother you?"

It kind of hit me that I was sitting on the grass with a famous outlaw. "No sir," I said, feeling strange.

"Now you *got* to get over that little hurdle, Cloudy. You can't go on calling me 'sir'!" He picked out a wild wheat stalk and started to suck it. "I won't rob a bank with somebody who treats me with respect. When it's time to light out, neither man should be holdin' the door open for the other, don't you see? There's a time when it's every man for hisself."

"Oh."

All of a sudden, I felt stiff inside. He kept looking at me, as though waiting for something more. I knew what he was waiting for, too. He wanted to know if I'd be his partner and help him rob the bank.

"Well, what about it, Cloudy?" His eyes were still on me, but they had changed into something hard. They didn't stop looking until they were part of the way into my head. It made me swallow.

"We in it together, son? We gonna take it?"

I couldn't talk. I guess I hadn't really believed that the old man—all white haired and dumpy looking who talked a blue streak—was an outlaw.

"Course, robbing a bank ain't like going to Sunday school. Don't ever let anybody tell you any different. It can get awful wild and woolly in a hurry, and you got to be up for it, when you go to rob a bank."

I couldn't seem to say anything, one way or the other. He waited, then he smiled at me, kind of disappointed, and struggled to his feet. "I see you ain't really up for it, son. I see where you'd rather think about it than do it." He jammed his hands in his pockets and pulled out a nickel. "Got a dime? So's I can have some pie with my coffee?"

"Wait." I had a dime, but wasn't going to give it to him, any more than I would call him a bad name. He wasn't some old bum off Skid Road. He was Kid Curry, a famous outlaw. "Wait a minute, Kid."

He turned, kind of tired, and looked at me. "Go on, boy."

It felt like I had just jumped off a cliff. "I'm up for it," I said.

SIX

You think you're up for it," Kid Curry said, staring at me, then looking at the nickel in his hand. All of a sudden he took that nickel and threw it a mile. "EEE-*YOW!*" he hollered. "We're gonna take a *bank*, boy. One more ride!" He pounded me on the back, like I'd made him proud in some way, then started prowling back and forth in front of the monkey cage. "First thing we got to do is make plans. Yessir. Ain't no substitute for plannin' ahead, is what Butch Cassidy always said."

"Butch Cassidy? Wasn't he an outlaw too?"

"He sure was, Cloudy, about the smartest outlaw God ever made. Course he was almighty finicky about his plans. He'd worry over the robbing of a bank the way a lawyer will worry over a 'whereas,' even when it looked like them bankers was just layin' the money on the counter, waitin' to be relieved of the responsibility of it. But one thing about Butch, he didn't get caught too often, even when things didn't come off

45

exactly the way he'd planned them to go. 'Contingencies.' Butch was a great one with words and he'd talk about contingency this and contingency that—I never was clear exactly on what it meant—but it worked for Butch, so we'll go ahead and make our plan big enough to account for one or two contingencies."

The Kid sure stored up a lot of words during his quiet period, I thought. But I kept it to myself.

"First thing we got to figure out is *when*," he said. "You can't just pack a picnic basket and then go rob a bank and then go off and have your picnic. No sir. You got to give yourself some time. . . . Now here's an idea. The Sheridan Rodeo is comin' up in about a month. That's a good time, maybe. Now let's take a look at it. The rodeo always starts on a Wednesday but the bank will be open in the morning, even though there ain't hardly anybody downtown in the morning because everybody is out at the fairgrounds. That's the best time to rob a bank, when there aren't too many dang fools around to worry about. How does that sound, Cloudy?"

I started to say something, but it was too late. He was talking again. "Too bad Tom O'Day ain't around." He stopped pacing back and forth and stared off into the distance, but I don't think he even saw what was right in front of him. "Tom was probably the most worthless bank robber that ever lived. One time, I believe it was in Torrington although it might have been Belle Fourche—no, it wasn't Belle Fourche but it wasn't Torrington, either—well, it don't matter. That dang fool Tom O'Day got so excited he clumb on his horse backwards. Now that was a 'contingency,' the way Butch explained it later. There was some advantage to it, too, because Tom could see who was a-comin' after us—but it slowed us down. Everybody got so tickled we could hardly ride. Fact is, we got caught—which was another 'contingency.' We only got sixty dollars and forty-two cents anyways, and you divide that up amongst five men and it don't even come out even—but we gave it all back and two days later, we escaped. Butch said we come out ahead by gettin' caught because we ate more'n sixty dollars and forty-two cents worth of food, but I never could see that particular line."

"Why do we need Tom O'Day?"

"Butch said if you could plan a robbery that even Tom could pull, it must be a pretty sound plan. Only reason I ever did see for keepin' that worthless little runt around. Another time he was a-holdin' the horses and after Sundance got mounted, why, Tom passed him the reins to the wrong horse. Sundance dug his spurs into one horse, you see, but was a-holdin' the reins to another, and he almost got pulled to the ground before he realized Tom's little mistake. It confused the posse though because with Sundance wheelin' around tryin' to stay on his mount, his horse spooked an' ran off in the wrong direction. Good thing for Tom. Sundance wanted to kill that crazy fool afterwards, but

Butch said if it hadn't happened that way, we'd probably gotten run down by that posse and hung. Butch said it proved something else, too, which is that God wanted us to rob that bank, and had the foresight to have Tom do the unexpected like he done. 'Foresight' was another of them words he tossed around that I never did exactly get the meaning of fixed in my mind. . . . Now *that* was Torrington. Yes. We got a hundred and fifteen dollars that time, which won't buy much whisky but will buy a lot of ice cream."

He sat down by the tree and picked up a needle and started working it in and out of his teeth. "Last I heard, Tom was in prison in Tennessee. Passed a bad check. Now if that ain't a come-down for a bank robber who rode with Butch Cassidy and the Wild Bunch, I don't know what is."

"What about our plan?"

"I'm thinkin' on it right now, I ain't just talkin' to hear myself talk. We need horses and saddles and enough provisions for a month. And we got to get them provisions cached above Fallen City, this pile of the strangest looking boulders you ever saw, which I know about up in the Big Horns, not more'n twenty miles from here. And I got to get a pistol, too." He looked at me. "No offense, Cloudy, but can you ride a horse?"

We used to have a stable in Denver, and I had a pony and would ride him all around. But whenever that horse and I were in the country, I'd get down and take off the saddle and let him follow. He was about the size of a dog anyway and it was easier on both of us with me walking. Then one day he got hit by a streetcar. "Sure can. I had a horse once."

"You don't say! A city feller like you and you had a horse! Well, at least I won't have to teach you how to ride." Then the excitement just kind of drained out of him, and he yawned. "I'm about wore out, Cloudy, with all this thinking and planning," he said. "I ain't worked this hard in one day in twenty years."

"All this work?" I asked, wondering what he was talking about.

"Yep," he said, then lumbered to his feet. He put his hands on his hips and arched his back, and I could hear it pop, just like knuckles. "Never figured on gettin' this old, either, son," he said. "Guess Butch'd call that a 'contingency.'"

The next day the Kid found some oats somewhere, and dug an old rope halter out of the monkey cage, and we started up Soldier Creek toward the Big Horns, looking for horses.

It sure was pretty when we started out, with those mountains off in the distance, but looming above us like clouds, and the sun nice and warm on my head. The Kid said we were on old man Jenkins's ranch, and that old man Jenkins wouldn't mind us riding his horses even if he knew about it, so it was just a waste of time to ask. It didn't sound exactly truthful, but I figured if we were going to rob a bank, a little thing like borrowing somebody's horse wouldn't hurt anything.

It turned out that hiking in the country wasn't one of the old man's strong points. About half a mile from town he handed me the halter, then came the sack with the oats, and about two miles out I noticed he wasn't hardly talking at all. He managed to say how surprised he was at Jenkins, who must have sold off all his horses, which was mighty shortsighted of him considering the economy, because the price of horses was sure to go back up—and then he stopped, even though he'd hardly warmed up to the subject. It was kind of a relief, in a way, but it had me worried, too. I'd sure like to have found some horses so we could quit walking. We'd seen some cattle grazing in the trees by the creek bed and on the hill near Soldier Creek Ditch, but no horses, and pretty soon it got so hot it even slowed down the mosquitoes. All you had to do was slosh around in the stream, which I did once or twice, but the Kid said he wouldn't because it wasn't dignified.

Not long after that he took a rest. That old hat of his was in his lap and his boots came off and his feet were hanging in a puddle of water—when he said, "Well, look over there." Four or five horses were grazing in a little clearing not more than a hundred yards away. Seeing them there, or else sitting down and cooling off his feet, started him right up talking again, and *that* was kind of a relief, too. "I tell you Cloudy, it's sure a comfort to know old man Jenkins ain't clear out of his head and hasn't sold off his whole herd. I thought we might have to hike all the way out to the PK Ranch, just to find a horse for you to practice on. Why at the slow pace things are a-goin', we might not get that bank robbed until 1936."

"I don't need any practice," I told him. "I can ride a horse."

"Without a saddle?"

"Gosh. I haven't ridden a horse without a saddle," I said.

"Then you'll need some practice, son. Forgot to mention one or two things. Borrowin' a horse is one thing but when you go to borrow a *saddle*, you can fetch yourself a whole barrel full of trouble. It ain't all that easy to ride a horse without a saddle, neither, and that's what takes the practice. But we just can't go around borrowin' saddles.

"You see, if a person ain't actually *on* his horse, and his horse is out to pasture, why then if the critter is gone, he won't miss it. But for some reason he'll still keep his eye on his saddle. Now if you was to take my saddle, for an example, I'd know about it in a minute, but if all you done was take my *horse* if I had a horse, which I ain't, but which if I did might be out grazin' in some pasture or other, why I wouldn't even miss him until I needed him and that might be a month. Now that's a peculiar thing but don't ever let anybody tell you they ain't a whole mountain full of things that's peculiar. In fact about the only thing a person can depend is that most things . . ."

"You mean I'll have to ride a horse without a saddle?"

He was fanning his face with that old sloppy hat. If he'd worked it any harder, it would have fallen apart. "That's what I mean, partner. We only got one saddle between us, which you ain't seen yet but which is back at my apartments, so to speak, and which I've had now about forty years; and it knows just where my bones are at and where they ain't and it fits me perfect. Don't look like much—I had to sell off the silver conchos a few years back to get out of jail—but when you're up in years like I am, and all them years has dragged your weight down to about your knees, it don't do to try to ride a horse bareback. You need a saddle, just to kind of hold things together."

Riding a horse without a saddle sounded like fun. "Is it hard?"

"Easy, once you get the hang of it. The best way for a young'n to ride, too, if you can just learn to get on. It's how the Indians ride all the time, except you'll see some rich ones—down in Oklahoma, where the gover'ment give 'em all that land with oil under it, then invented cars—and they'll put a saddle on a horse and kind of strut when they ride, like a white man with a new car. They'll get an expression on their face, like this—" his chin went up and his mouth clamped shut and he looked like my father does sometimes when he's tasting wine—"and they don't look like it, but it makes them feel better. The Indians around here ride bareback because they're so poor they can't afford saddles. Besides . . ."

"How do you get on?" I asked.

"Well, that's the trick, all right. If somebody's around you can get a lift, but when you're off by yourself you got to get your horse over by a stump and climb on that way, or the way the Indians do, they jump. Now you take them ponies over there. We ain't wastin' time sittin' here, by the way. Can't stand to waste time, I need to be busy every minute, so I'm glad we're busy here restin' and talkin' too and lettin' them critters get used to us. The little gray that's closest to us looks about right. She's small and looks friendly and curious, and in a minute or two I want you to take them oats and that halter I brung . . . Know how to handle a halter?"

I looked at it. The ring for the nose looked big enough to go over an elephant. "If she won't take that, she won't take anything," I said.

"You just slip it on her and bring her over here."

I took the oats and halter and walked toward the ponies slow and easy, because I didn't want to get them running. The big roan laid his ears back and moved away, but when I jiggled the oats, he looked interested. For a minute I thought I might be in a whole crowd of horses, so I bee-lined for the gray mare and the rest of them watched, but left us alone.

The mare nuzzled up like she knew me, and I gave her a whole handful of oats. Then she waited for me to put the halter on—I didn't have to trick her or anything—and she even jiggled her head a little so it would ride back over her ears. She didn't complain at all when I took hold of the halter rope and led her away.

What the Kid didn't know was that I have a way with horses and dogs. My father used to say they liked me because I wasn't any kind of threat to them, I had the same mentality. I think he was teasing when he said that, but I never knew for sure.

"Say," the Kid said after I'd led the gray to where he was resting. "Now you cut that horse out and catched her about as easy as I ever see anybody do. I named you right, Cloudy. That other little feller I told you about? He was the same way. Why, you'd've thought he could speak horse!"

"She sure is nice," I said. "You think she'll let me ride her?"

"Why, I think she *wants* you to ride her. Look how she's moving into you. Why, I think that horse is in love!" He laughed and swatted his knees with his hat, and I thought it would tear but it didn't. Then he got to his feet. "Now if you had a saddle you'd probably want a bridle, just to give that horse something to chew on. But maybe that rope halter'll be enough. I reckon it'll have to be, in fact, because we ain't got a spare bridle. Lemme have some oats." I gave him the bag. "All right, horse," he said, and dug out a handful. "I'm Kid Curry and I'm a mean and dangerous outlaw, but I ain't gonna hurt you and you don't need to be afraid. You understand?" She understood, all right. She laid her ears back but didn't lean away, then reached for the oats, working her lips over them and drawing them into her mouth. "Nice horse," the Kid said, rubbing the bone over her nose. "Nice horse." She let him rub, but she kept her eyes on him, too.

"All right, Cloudy, I reckon she knows us good enough, so up you go." He got beside her and made a stirrup out of his hands. "Now just give me your left foot—thataway—now grab onto something that belongs to that horse, like a ear or her mane, it don't matter much what—thataway—and up you *go*—uh oh. Whao-a-ao, horse! *Whoa!*"

For such a little horse, she sure could run! The next thing I knew she was tearing across that clearing and headed for Soldier Creek Ditch, and I was wrapped around her hanging on for dear life! I hadn't even gotten ahold on the reins, which were just an old rope that hung off the halter. Every time she reached forward with her front legs I thought they'd get tangled up in that dang rope. But they never did and I finally got my hands on the reins and pulled them in. By the time we reached the ditch, that old mare stretched over the whole thing as easy as stepping over a crack in the sidewalk.

It was scary, but it sure was fun. I looked at her ears and they were up as straight as the hackles on the back of a cat. That *horse* was having fun, too! She kept on running across the open grassland west of the ditch and then I got my knees into her and sat up, holding onto the reins. I tugged at them, pulling her head back, and she was ready to quit anyhow, so she stopped.

Sometimes I'll laugh after a good scare, and I laughed so hard I almost fell off her back. "You sure are a funny horse," I told her, working my hand up and down the mane on her neck. She liked it, and moved her head back and forth to get the full benefit of my hand. "You need a name, though. Some ways, you're like my mother—" it really felt good to talk to that horse and know she understood me—"so you know what? I'm gonna call you Dot. Your real name is 'Dorothy,' but nobody calls you that. Some people call you 'Dottie,' but that sounds like you're not exactly right in the head.

"So come on, Dot. Let's go find the Kid."

SEVEN

There's a whole lot more to robbing a bank than I thought. I'd sure have made a mess of it if I'd tried it by myself. The way the Kid explained it, the robbing part is easy. The real problem is getting away.

"Settin' up a hide-out in them mountains above Fallen City ain't no waste of time at all, Cloudy," he told me. "Once you start in a-runnin', it's a comfort to know you've got a place to go. Now you take Hole-in-the-Wall. When me and Butch and Sundance and that dang fool Tom O'Day was at our busiest back before there was telephones and telegraphs in every blessed little town—which put an awful strain on our business, I'll tell you that, because then a posse could be a-comin' *toward* you just as well as from behind—before that happened, why after we'd make a with-drawal from a bank, like as not we'd head for Hole-in-the-Wall, where there was food and water and bunks. That way we didn't have to pack so much, and

I'll tell you this, too. After you've had your pistol up against some banker's nose, and the whole country is a-chasin' after you, why it's just plain an advantage to be travelin' light.

"Course we didn't always go to Hole-in-the-Wall. If we was down in Colorado we'd probably head for Robber's Roost, and to tell the truth, I preferred the Roost. The neighbors was more friendly, most of them being thieves too, you see, but that was awful poor country down in there, which put banks in short supply, and not many trains. The banks and trains down there got pretty well worked over. But there was good grass and water and some wild steers so we could eat some civilized meat now and then, 'stead of venison, which tastes like it's been dipped in turpentine to a white man although the Indians prefer it, or squirrel, which is hardly worth buildin' a fire for unless you can trap five or six of the little varmints. And you can never depend on the taste of a squirrel. Why, squirrels from the same family—brothers and sisters—will taste as different as popcorn and peanuts. The only way to even out the taste is to layer the meat over with about a inch of salt, which is fine if you happen to like salt and are near a lake, because using the right proportions for squirrel tends to build up your thirst, though I never could develop a taste for salt. But I've known . . ."

He sure could talk. He could talk for miles at a time and sometimes I was afraid he'd get so interested in what he was talking about he'd forget to breathe, and suffocate.

In about a week we had pretty near filled up the monkey cage with enough provisions for a safari into Africa, all of it slated for our hide-out in the Big Horns. Most of it was stuff Grandmother Galdbreath wouldn't miss, such as a quilt and a wool blanket and a pillowcase to put things in. The Kid told me to take the pillowcase back because a gunnysack'd work just as well. I also took some coffee and beans and a slab of bacon and some salt and baking powder and flour, and a knife and a fork.

She missed the knife and fork. She kind of wondered about that bacon, too. Anyway, she looked perplexed, coming out of the cooler, and said, "I *swear!*" But she didn't go on and on about it like she did the knife and fork. "What has happened to my silverware?" she wondered, and it made me nervous. The mistake I'd made was taking it from the fancy box she kept in the dining room, that I thought she never opened. When she came to me about it, I decided I'd better find it to keep her from noticing the other stuff.

"You mean the knives and forks and spoons that are in that box?"

"Yes. Have you seen it? The girls are coming over Tuesday and I only have eight place settings as it is!"

"Some of it's in my room, Grandmother. I had a piece of pie and I guess I forgot . . ."

"But a fork and a *knife* are missing. You took the knife too?"

"Yes'm."

"For pie?"

I almost told her I needed it because the crust was so thick, which would have been a mistake because she'd have been insulted, so instead I told her I needed it to put the peanut butter on with.

"Peanut butter? On your pie?"

"It's really good that way, Grandmother." I'd done the same thing one time when my father missed a pipe. I told him I needed it to blow soap bubbles with, and he laughed. So instead of giving me a lecture and a spanking, he rumpled my hair. "Makes the pie kind of chewy."

She rumpled my hair. "Wait'll I tell the girls. You run up to your room and . . ."

"Could I get it when I get back from the movie? It starts in five minutes."

"Oh, all right. Here, you'll need a quarter."

So it worked out better than I'd thought. I had time to get the silverware back to the house, and got an extra quarter, too.

Then on Tuesday, which was on the ninth of July and the rodeo was only eight days off, me and the Kid made packs out of gunnysacks and hauled the supplies out to Soldier Creek. It was only a mile and we started out walking fast, but it finally took a whole hour and a half. The Kid had a sunstroke on the way and would

60

have died if we hadn't traded packs. Then he left that one too and I had to come back for it. "We'll make it, Cloudy," he said. "Not much further now and if I wasn't so near death, I could help you with that pack, but I can see you don't need help and I wouldn't want to offend you by offerin'."

I was pretty tired by that time, and it wouldn't have bothered me at all.

"I hid my saddle in that tree just last night, which is probably why I'm all wore out and tired today. That's the place to hide a saddle, too, just for future reference, in case you ever need to hide one. Not too many cowboys would think to look in a tree for a saddle and as heavy as it is, I don't know how in tarnation I got it out here either, or up in that tree. It just went up there like it was a feather. Course I'd had a little wine, which helps to take away the pain now and then, and could be why I'm feelin' so poorly today, but last night was just a pure pleasure."

I got the packs under the tree and looked up, and sure enough, up in a crotch between some branches was the old man's saddle. He'd already sat down under the tree and had taken his hat off and was working his back into that tree like it was a sofa. "You just go on off now and fetch that little mare of yours while I rest up, and take that rope off your pack and see if you can catch me an animal too. Don't need anything fancy like a racehorse or a trotter, just a plain old horse, big enough to carry me and pull that little mare of yours. And don't worry none about me neither even though like as not I'll be a poor old corpse by the time you get back." His eyes closed and his legs, which were stretched out in front of him, had that loose look like they'd fallen asleep. "Life can be a burden anyways when you get old and fat if you ain't rich. Course I wasn't always fat. Used to be thin as a broom handle, but . . . " He started in breathing heavy, so I figured he'd be all right.

It took me an hour to catch my mare and then when I started giving oats to an old red that had seen better days but looked big enough, it made Dot jealous, which caused some trouble. But I finally got the rope over the red and climbed Dot, and we got back to where the old man was sleeping. He'd made pillows out of the packs and was still as a rock. He said he'd be dead and he looked like it, but at least he'd died happy because there was a smile on his face—when he opened his mouth and vacuumed in about three yards of air. Then he let it out like a tidal wave.

If there'd been any flies in the vicinity of the old man, they'd have been goners. . . . Then I couldn't seem to help myself. I tethered the horses in a grassy place near the creek and found some dandelions that had gone to seed but hadn't lost their thistles, and blew them into the air not far from where he was sleeping. He dragged in all that sky, and they headed for his mouth like water down a drain.

I've learned since that thistles on the lung can be

fatal, but I didn't know that then. At first the expression on his face, when it changed from good dream to curious, struck me as funny, and when it went from there to disaster, I started to laugh. But then he got to gagging and coughing and couldn't get his breath. When his face went from red to white to green, I thought he was going to die, and it scared me bad. I thumped him on the back hard enough to break down a door, and he finally coughed them out or swallowed them all the way down, one or the other.

I was close to crying by the time he was done. I told him how sorry I was, and I meant it, too. He'd taught me how to ride bareback—or at least arranged things so I taught myself—and we were partners, up for robbing a bank.

"Dang you anyway, Cloudy!" he said when it was all over. "You sure have got a different kind of streak. Like Kid . . . I mean, Sundance."

"Who?"

"Kid Sundance. The Sundance Kid. Just quiet-like for days at a time, lulling people into thinking nothing at all is turnin' through your mind, and then busting out like a chunk of lightning." He got up and slapped his hat against his leg, and put it on. "But I get the point," he said, looking at me like I'd taught him a lesson. "Guess maybe I'll carry my own pack from now on."

EIGHT

It took forever to get Dot loaded with all the gear I'd stolen from Grandmother Galdbreath, but we finally got it done so it would stay on her. Then the Kid put his saddle on that old red. He said he felt vigorous enough to ride clear to Fallen City and back in one day, after getting himself rinsed out with all them thistles. Then he waved good-bye, dragging Dot along like she was a log and kicking that old plowhorse about three times for each step. I watched them plug along up Soldier Creek for the Big Horns, then started to walk back to town.

He didn't make it that day, though. I hung around the monkey cage for as long as I could, then returned after dinner and stayed until it got dark, just in case.

The next morning I checked the monkey cage first thing, but he wasn't there. I went over to the barber shop and read all the comic books, then ran back to the monkey cage but he still wasn't there. It kind of made my stomach hurt. The rodeo started in a week, so he'd have to hurry if we were going to get that bank robbed on schedule. I hung around for as long as I could stand it, then picked some flowers and took them to Miss Landusky. Maybe she would give me a piece of pie.

"Alex, how nice!"

"Yes'm."

She opened the screen door and took the flowers out of my hand and told me to get in quick before all the flies in the county found out the door was open. She'd been reading, and I could see where the spectacles had pinched her nose. "Well now," she said after sticking the flowers in a vase and fluffing them some kind of way. "Sit down and tell me what you've been doing."

I didn't want to give her a heart attack, so I didn't tell her the truth. "Fishing I guess, and swimming. I saw Mickey Mouse three times."

"Could I interest you in a piece of pie?"

"Pie?"

"Oh. Well, if you'd rather not . . ."

"I guess it would be all right."

"Shall I bring some peanut butter too?"

"Peanut butter! What for?"

"For the pie. Mildred tells me . . ."

"Oh." I'd forgotten all about that. "Well, that's only good on certain kinds."

"I've some apple pie. Is it good on apple?"

"No'm, it's terrible."

She smiled in a funny way and I had the feeling she could see right through me. Still, she brought the biggest piece of pie I'd ever seen, and it was delicious. I ate it in about five seconds.

"Did you come over here just to get a piece of pie?"

I gulped. The truth is I'd started to feel a little mean when I saw how glad she was to see me. "I was hoping you'd give me some, Miss Landusky, but I like to talk to you, too."

I could tell that made her feel better. "Are you getting ready for the rodeo?"

"I guess so. Haven't decided whether to go."

"You *must* go to the rodeo. Everyone goes. Even the Indians come down for it—in spite of the fact they aren't always made to feel welcome."

I'd heard about the Indians but hadn't seen any around town. "Where do they live, Miss Landusky?"

"Just north of here, in Montana, the Cheyenne and the Crows. The Crows have the largest reservation. It includes the battleground where General Custer had his famous 'Last Stand'—even though the Crows had very little to do with that fight. They were on Custer's side. The Cheyenne were the ones who fought against him."

"Where do the Cheyenne Indians live?" I asked.

"Just east of the Crows, along the Tongue River."

"I'd like to shoot me an Indian," I said, trying to sound like the men I'd heard in the barber shop.

But she didn't like it. In fact, it made her mad. "You

don't really feel that way, young man. Why should you talk that way? The Indians are *people*. They are entitled to your respect as much as anyone—in spite of what you may hear in this town."

It kind of surprised me. "Yes'm."

Later on, she told me about the book she was reading, written by a Russian and all about a bunch of Russians—and she'd read it before, so I couldn't understand why she'd go to all the trouble to read it again. Something about "old friends," was the way she explained it. Somehow after that we started talking about my mom.

Miss Landusky had really liked my mother—my real mother, not the one I had now—and was quite certain that if I'd said something about shooting Indians to *her*, I'd have been holding my behind afterward, trying to soothe it. "You can be proud of your mother, Alex. She had the courage to stand up for what she believed in, and that can get difficult in a town the size of Sheridan. But I've never met your father. Tell me about him."

"He's okay. Except . . ."

"Except what?"

I didn't really want to talk about my father. "The only time he knows I'm around is when I do something wrong."

"I see," she said. "He's very successful, isn't he?"

"Yes'm."

"And I suppose he'd like you to be a success, too?"

"I don't know. I think he'd like me out of his hair."

"Well." She patted her chest with her hand. "Why do you think that?"

"He wouldn't even take me to Paris, France."

"Well," she said again, patting her temple with her hand this time. "And you feel he should have taken you?"

"If my real mom was alive, they would have."

Something went wrong with my face, and I kind of started to snuffle. Dang it, I thought.

"Come sit by me, Alex. You're too far away."

I got up and went over to the couch, where she was sitting. I opened my eyes real wide, which was a trick I'd learned to keep from crying. Then she put her arm around me and pulled me toward her, which didn't help. I had to open my mouth real wide, too.

"Now. I want you to tell me about your step-mother."

"She's okay. If she didn't pat me on the head and talk babytalk."

"But the two of them go off on trips in the summer and send you to Sheridan. Is that it?"

"Yes'm."

"Do you know why they don't take you?"

"My dad says it's because my voice hasn't changed."

"Well," she said, for the third time. "I'll bet when it does, you won't want to go with them anyway."

"Sure I will! What difference will that make?"

"You'll have your own things to do then. Just as they have their own things to do now."

I looked up at her, wondering what she was talking about. She was smiling, but some tears were leaking out of her eyes. It really surprised me.

"You don't need to move if you don't want to, Alex. I'm quite comfortable."

"I'm not." I wanted to run to the other side of the room. But she'd really been nice, so I stayed where I was but kind of moved away. She lifted her arm. Then I thought of something I'd been meaning to ask. "What does 'renegade' mean?"

She let her hand drop on my neck and rubbed it, and it felt so good that after a while I didn't even notice. " 'Renegade'? Something like outlaw. Or outsider. Why do you ask?"

I told her some men at the barber shop had been talking about a "renegade Indian."

"That would be Arosho, I expect."

"Who?"

"Arosho, an Indian who has gone bad. I knew him when he was your age, perhaps ten years ago, when I was doing mission work on the Crow reservation. He's the son of a great Crow warrior."

"Does he rob banks or something?"

"No, he isn't that kind of outlaw. He fights a lot—which isn't terrible, except if you happen to be an Indian who fights white men." She sounded miffed

can't handle one Indian, we shouldn't be robbin'
banks."

Then he crawled into his "rooms," which is what
he called the monkey cage sometimes, where it was
cool. "Come by in the morning, will you, son?" he
asked, poking his head out the door. "Might see if you
can bring me some pie."

NINE

The day before the rodeo it was hot enough to fry ants on the sidewalk, and the only thing I could stand was short pants. When I got to Kendrick Park I even peeled off my shoes and socks, then went looking for the Kid. He was sitting on the grass in front of the monkey cage.

I don't know where he got that pistol, but he had one on. He had long pants on, too, and heavy boots, and a hat, and still he looked cool. At first I thought something was wrong with him. Instead of saying hello the way he usually did, he hardly noticed me, just kept chewing on a match. The expression on his face was different, too. It was crinkly, like he was waiting for something to happen, but if it did, he believed he could handle it. And his eyes wouldn't focus on anything. They were open and I could tell he could see everything there was to see, but they looked like mirrors, or the eyes of a rattlesnake while it's still coiled.

"Hi, Kid," I said, expecting him to start talking the way he usually did, which was like a train.

"Cloudy."

A cricket started over his leg and without even looking at it, he flicked it a mile. Then he sat there still and easy, like a spider in a web, ready for whatever might happen next.

"Aren't you hot with all those clothes on?"

"Nope."

Usually with an opener like that he'd start talking and sometimes he wouldn't have noticed if I were to leave and go around the block. I thought he was sick. "You all right?"

"Yup."

I hunkered down in the shade of a tree and wriggled my toes into the grass to keep them cool. "Can I see your gun?"

His eyes lost their blank look and kind of thumped me with a stare, and it almost knocked me over. Then, real slow, he reached down and pulled the gun out of the holster, flipped his hand some way, and was holding it by the barrel. He handed it to me, butt first. "It's loaded, Cloudy," he said. "Leave it that way."

The barrel looked to be about a foot long, but it was really shorter than that. I didn't try to break it open or spin the cylinder where the cartridges were, but just twisted it in my hand and felt it. It sure was heavy. I could tell it'd been kept clean with oil. "Neat," I said. "Can I shoot it?"

He snorted air through his nose, like he thought that was funny. "Don't mean to hurt your feelings, Cloudy, but she might tear off your arm. You need to grow a little first." When I handed it back he did something fancy with it, then eased it into his holster and sat there, all still again, and waiting.

After a while, I left. He didn't seem to want me around. Besides, everything was ready. We had a hideout and horses, and the Kid even had a gun.

I found out something else about robbing a bank, too. The hardest part is trying to sleep the night before you do it.

I was up by six in the morning and too nervous to eat anything. I could hear Grandmother Galdbreath snoring away, so I stuck a note on the kitchen table that told her I'd be at the rodeo that day "with James," who was a friend I'd invented to explain where I'd been spending all my time. Then I took off for Soldier Creek, just the way we had it planned. I had to get the horses and bring them in.

It was really nice outside. The sun had been up about an hour but the moon still hung on the other end of the sky, with nothing but blue sky and mountains in between. I could hear the frogs and crickets along the creek bed. They'd stop as I got near, then start up again as I went by, so I was a thing in the center with sounds all around me. But by the time I got back to town with the horses, the sun was higher and you

he whispered. "Somebody might recognize me. Fact is, I think I'll mosey on back to the monkey cage. We'll just have to wait a spell, Cloudy, before we go to rob that bank. You come get me when this dang fool parade is over." He pulled his hat down and started off, then stopped. "What was it you asked?"

"Everybody I see with a gun has it strapped onto their leg, and I just wondered how come you don't?"

He scoffed. "I bet they think they are bad. Yessir. I bet they think they are bad men who just might have to shoot their way out of town. But I bet there ain't a one of 'em could shoot his way out of a paper bag. Why if they was to ride a horse with their iron tied down that way, it'd bounce out of their holster quicker'n they'd get bucked off the horse, but mine'd stay right where it is, and flop against my hip, and if it came out, why at least I'd know it." Then he looked both ways, kind of like he was checking behind his back, and shuffled out of sight.

I walked over to the sidewalk, relieved as could be that we weren't ready to rob that bank yet. He'd said you have to be up for it when you go to rob a bank, and with him acting funny, I wasn't up for it. I started nosing my way through to the curbing so I could see the parade. "Alex?" somebody said.

It was Miss Landusky, standing a little away from everybody else like she usually did, and all dressed up and wearing a hat.

80

"Yes'm."

"Who was that man you were talking to?" She looked peculiar sort of, like she was pretty sure she'd seen something happen that was impossible.

"That was—well, he didn't tell me his name. He wanted to know where the hotel was." My gosh, I thought. Had she recognized the Kid?

"I'd swear I've seen that man," she said, her head over to one side, as if she was thinking. "Well. It will come to me. So you're here to watch the parade."

"Yes'm."

"I've watched every parade in Sheridan for the last thirty years and have always managed a front row seat. Will you join me?"

"Yes'm," I said, trying to keep my voice from shaking. What if she'd recognized him? I asked myself. I'd have to warn him! "Who did you think that man was, Miss Landusky?" I asked. "A dangerous outlaw?"

She laughed. "No. A harmless one, if you can imagine such a thing. With a scheme of some kind always in his mind. Some were quite clever—in fact, too clever. Most of them failed miserably."

We went right on by the knots of people on Main and turned up Fifth. Hardly anybody was on Fifth Street at all. I felt a lot better, knowing she hadn't realized the man she had seen was her old boyfriend. "Well who, Miss Landusky?" I asked. "Butch Cassidy?"

"Heavens, child. You're reminding me of things I thought I'd forgotten. Not Butch." She smiled in that young way again. "His schemes worked."

"Probably not even an outlaw," I said, kind of hopefully.

"Oh yes, if he's the fellow I'm thinking of, he was an outlaw. He was in the Wild Bunch with the rest of them, although he wasn't very wild."

That gave me a scare. Maybe she knew after all. "What was his name?"

"Tom something or other." She thought a moment. "Tom O'Day?"

"My gosh."

"Alex, what's wrong?"

"I stubbed my toe." We kept on walking until we got to the bridge that crossed Big Goose, and stopped just on the other side. "You sure it wasn't one of the others?"

"What is going through that head of yours! As a matter of fact, I'm not sure at all. I hardly saw the man, and time does terrible things to one's body. I really don't know who it was."

It looked like everybody in Sheridan had turned out to watch the parade, and half an hour later, after it warmed up another twenty degrees, there were people spread along the curbing of Fifth Street, too. Miss Landusky said the parade had to go that way to get to the fairground. Then everyone started craning their

82

necks toward Main. "Here they come!" somebody yelled.

I could hardly see, I was so busy thinking, because what if that old man was really Tom O'Day? It sure would explain a lot. . . . But how could it be? I'd heard the old man talk about Tom O'Day, and as near as I could tell, he didn't even like him. Then the parade got started, and it was awful hard not to watch.

First came the soldiers from Fort Sheridan, carrying the colors, and marching real smart to the rhythm of a drum and fife. They'd go forward and backward and "Mark time, *march!*" which meant walk without going anywhere, and the ones with rifles would slap them around in exactly the same way. Those soldiers from the fort just bristled and when they got to the bridge their feet, working together, sounded like a drum, and that old bridge started to sway. When they passed in front of us the Lieutenant called out, "Eyes *right!*" and they all turned and looked at Miss Landusky, which was more than they'd done for the mayor.

Lagging along after the soldiers came the Sheridan Baseball Team. The way they marched was sure a contrast to the army. They'd skip around in circles and sometimes let out a war whoop, each man doing whatever he felt like, and the only way you could tell they were together was because they wore the same uniform. People lined along the sidewalk would yell at one of them and whoever it was would trot over and talk a while, then get back with the group when the notion struck him. Sheridan had already lost fifteen games out of twenty-two, and the way some of the men were drinking whisky, I didn't expect them to win any more that week.

A band of Indians came after the baseball players, and most of the people on the sidewalk just stared at them. About five of the Indians were on horseback, two with bonnets of feathers that hung clear down to their waists. Some braves wearing only breechcloths, with some squaws decked out in deerskin, walked in a knot in the middle. I asked Miss Landusky why everything got so quiet, and she whispered to me that they were Crows, and that Arosho had boasted he'd come to the rodeo. When they got next to us one of the chiefs looked at Miss Landusky and gave her a sort of salute, and she smiled at him and nodded her head. "Was that him?" I asked.

"Gracious no. He'd be recognized in the parade. That was Poporan, whom I've known many years."

"You teach him English when you worked on the reservation?"

"Actually, he taught me much more than I taught him."

"That old Indian? I bet he can't even read."

"Oh, he can read, all right. Just from looking at you, I wouldn't be surprised but what he knows you better than your father does."

"*That* wouldn't be hard." She laughed and shook

her head, which she did a lot around me. "You think Arosho'll come to the rodeo?" I asked.

"I hope not. I certainly hope not."

"Why not, Miss Landusky? If he does, maybe they'll catch him."

"They'd do more than that. Half the men in town will be drunk before very much longer, and feeling quite festive, probably. If he were caught today, he'd get lynched. And . . . Oh, I don't know."

"Don't know what?"

"He's supposed to have killed a man, a woman, and a child, but no one saw him do it, and I just can't believe Arosho would murder a small child." *That* put a chill in my back. Then Miss Landusky smiled again in that funny way. "It's a terrible thing to say I suppose, but as long as it's been done, I hope he's the one who did it."

"Why? You just got done saying he couldn't have!"

"Because even if he didn't, he'll hang for it."

She sure was a different old lady. Sometimes I thought it wouldn't even surprise her if she knew I was going to rob the bank.

Some floats were going by, just as fancy as any I'd ever seen in Denver. They were full of flowers and girls and messages like "Land of the Free," and "From Wilderness to Bounty," and "Victory at Wounded Knee," and except for Miss Landusky, people cheered and whistled and clapped when they passed. A covered wagon pulled by the two biggest oxen I'd ever seen got wedged in between the last two floats, and the animals were so big and wild looking I thought they might be part buffalo. Then along came some more Indians and behind them the sheriff's posse, mounted on horses. In a way it looked like the cavalry was chasing the Indians down the street.

"Those are the Cheyenne," Miss Landusky said. " 'Cheyenne' means 'Tall People,' and they certainly are. Even the short ones."

She said things like that all the time, things you could understand sort of, even though they didn't make sense. But she was right. Somehow those Indians looked to be a few inches taller than they really were. They weren't sort of squat looking like the Crows, or maybe it was just the way they walked, which was springy and high—except for one who walked in the careful way of the Crows, like he was on a path in the mountains, stalking a deer. He didn't look any taller than he was. "What about him?" I asked, and pointed.

Real quick, some Indians closed around the one I'd pointed at, but Miss Landusky saw him and sucked in her breath. Then he broke through the knot and walked toward us. He stared at Miss Landusky a minute like there was something he wanted her to understand, and she stared back with eyes that were sad. Slowly he raised his hand, palm down, to his waist and held it there. Then he made some kind of gesture, and walked away.

"Golly. Was that Arosho?"

She looked at me with the same sad eyes. "No."

The bank closed at twelve, so there wasn't much time. I got away from Miss Landusky as soon as I could and ran over to Kendrick Park to get the Kid.

He took his saddle out and we lugged it to the end of the park where the horses were tethered. Then we mounted up and rode down Loucks Street toward the bank. My stomach felt like it was full of bees, which is the way my dad had told me his felt when he went off to war. It sure was exciting, but I wasn't sure how much excitement I could stand. I wanted to hurry up and get it over with.

"Now you know what to do don't you, Cloudy?" the Kid asked me for the twentieth time, so I guessed he was as nervous and excited as me. "You know exactly what to do don't you, son? I'll be dependin' on you and if you don't do it exactly the way we planned, why the whole thing will come down right on top of us and we'll go to jail for twenty years or get killed, and you're too young and I'm too old for *either* of those things to happen over a simple miscalculation." Usually his voice would roll along like a slow moving train but today it skittered around like a rabbit. "Now you got to hold my horse by the reins and saddle horn and keep her steady, 'cause when I come out of that there bank, I'll be a-runnin'! You can count on that! Now remember I load from the left so that means you got to be on the right, clear out of the way. That's right now, ain't it? Let's see. If you're on the west side of that door—or do I mean on the east side?—well you must do it *right*, Cloudy. Dang. Wish Butch was here. He'd know right away without even thinkin' which side of the door you should be on, and I knew it yesterday but it seems to have slid out of my mind, what with worryin' so about gettin' a young boy like you all mixed up into a life of crime."

Then all of a sudden he stopped his horse and the pucker went out of his forehead. "That must be it," he said, and a big smile spread over his face. "Yessir. I'm all worry and conscience and morals over it. Ain't got a thing to do with what *I* want to do—if I could do it alone I'd say let 'er on out of the chute, boys, 'cause ain't anything goin' to buck *me* off!—but what's botherin' me is taking you down the chute too.

"A boy like you, a fine young man whose father is rich and who has his whole life stretched out in front. Am I goin' to be the one to ruin it for him? No sir! Cloudy, it's off. It ain't right to get you mixed up into a thing like this and spend the rest of your life wonderin' if that tap on your shoulder means back to jail for another twenty year. Now if I was alone that'd be . . ."

It made me mad. "You want to quit?" I asked him,

butting in. "I thought you were Kid Curry. He wouldn't quit!"

"What?"

"Miss Landusky thinks you're Tom O'Day!"

It took his breath away, and it did the same to mine. "*That* little runt!" he said, after a minute. "Well, I can tell you this, son, I *am* Kid Curry and I *ain't* Tom O'Day. I just wanted to give you one final chance to back out."

"I don't want to back out, " I said, and I didn't, either.

He nodded and started forward on his horse. That old leather saddle went "shh, shh, shh," and those sounds played along with the "clop, clop, clop" of the red horse's shoes. Maybe you got enough nerve for both of us, Cloudy," he said. "I might have lost a piece of mine about twenty year ago, and then settin' in that monkey cage just now, waitin' for it to happen, and thinkin' of all the things that can go wrong . . ."

Then his mood just took a turn. "*Eeeeee* HAH!" he yipped, and whipped off his hat and slapped that old red's flank. "Come on Cloudy, we got to hurry! What if they was to close that bank before we could get there?"

But the bank was still open, and there wasn't a soul except for us on the street.

So the conditions were right, just the way we'd planned it.

TEN

The Big Horns off in the distance looked cool, like purple icebergs, but the sun beat down on the top of my head at about a hundred degrees. That old man had been in there too long. Dot kept moving around under me like she was floating down a stream, and trying to stay on top of that horse and keep the Kid's big red steady at the same time was hard to do.

Then the door to the bank flew open, and there he was! He had a gunnysack in one hand and his pistol in the other and he was waving them both around like they were snakes. "*Wah-ooo-way* YEOW!" he hollered, then aimed his pistol at the sun and cranked off a couple of shots. That was just what Old Red needed. He went up on his hind legs like a bear climbing a tree and it pretty near lifted me all the way off Dot. "Whoa-oa now boy, easy," I said, and the horse gentled a little and then the Kid blew another hole in the air. That time Old Red went up on his front legs and Dot started squirting around like a wet piece of soap. I was stretched between them like a bridge made out of rope. "Hold him nice and steady now, Cloudy, 'cause here I come!"

The Kid got his foot in the stirrup and grabbed the saddle horn, but swung up so hard he almost sailed clear over his horse and across the street. Later on when I thought about it I laughed, but at the time I was too busy trying to get out of his way. "Yippee Yah Hah Wah Dee Doodle!" he shouted and somehow landed in the saddle with the reins in his hand. His horse did the rest. Old Red took off down Main as hard as he could go, like he was trying to stay in front of a flood.

But one of the things I noticed right away was that we were riding off in the wrong direction. Oh no, I thought, because it was the kind of mistake Tom O'Day would make! We had planned to go south on Main Street until we were out of town, then cut through Greg Draw over to Big Goose. We were on Main all right, but headed north toward Montana, instead of south toward our hideout in the Big Horns!

I kept hollering at him to stop, but he just leaned forward on Old Red and kept slapping him with the reins. But at Fifth Street he suddenly turned around in his saddle and shouted, "Cloudy, we're a-headed the wrong way!" Then he turned left, which would take us out of town going west.

At least the Big Horns were in that general direction,

but the trouble was, that road took us right by the fairgrounds, where all the people had gone to watch the rodeo. When we galloped by, the old outlaw felt so good that he pointed his gun at the only cloud in the sky and put three holes in it.

"Move, boy, *move!*" he yelled at me, but he didn't need to. Me and Dot had started gaining on him and Old Red. We were out of town by that time, on Soldier Creek Road, which was an old dirt highway that went to Fort Sheridan where the soldiers stayed. But when he looked back, his face fell. "Oh my goodness, Cloudy, we are in trouble now! There's a posse after us!"

"My gosh," I said, turning around and looking at the huge cloud of dust that boiled up off the ground. "A posse?"

"Dang it, how'd we get over here by the fairgrounds?" He yanked off his hat and used it to whip his horse with. "Ride, boy, ride!"

The riders behind us looked like shadows against a cloud of yellow smoke. I was really scared. I didn't want to get caught! I leaned over Dot and tried to get her to run faster, because if she'd wanted, we could have left Old Red and the Kid like they were rooted to the ground. But Dot wouldn't do it. She got right behind that old horse and kind of pushed him along.

Then somebody in that posse started shooting at us! Man oh man, I thought, what have I gotten myself into! All I did was rob a bank! But the noise from the guns even got Old Red's interest, and instead of plodding along like he was pulling a plow, he started running like he was being chased by a lion. "Oh-h-h Gol dang it," the old man squeaked. The way it was going, I started thinking he was Tom O'Day for sure, instead of a real bad man. He was bent over his horse like a jockey coming down the stretch, his big rear end way up in the air and his face down where he couldn't see, like an ostrich. "Them people are a-shootin' at us, Cloudy, real bullets! A poor old man and an innocent child, and for what? A gunnysack full of paper! That's what!" He sounded grieved over it, like he couldn't believe the meanness of those people, but I thought, If I had a gun, I'd shoot you myself!

The road we were riding on was flat as a pancake and I could see through the dust that they were only five hundred yards behind. I counted four of them. It was a good thing they kept on shooting, in a way, because Old Red would start to slow down, and then they'd crank off a shot and off he'd go again, like an explosion. It still looked like they were gaining on us, though. The road started through the draw toward Soldier Creek, and about then is when the Kid seemed to give up. "Five miles to go, son, just to get up into the mountains! If we could fly we might have a chance, but it don't look good." He sounded almost peaceful about it. "Don't you worry none though, boy. I'll tell 'em I forced you to come with me and . . ."

Just then an army truck from a little dirt side road

swung onto the road behind us and got between us and that posse. It churned up more dust than twenty horses and it was like the posse had disappeared. When I looked back all I could see was a man with a face that looked like a rock, sitting next to the driver of the truck. He was in a uniform with medals clear across his chest, and I figured he must be the general of the whole world. "Now they even got the army after us, Cloudy, we might as well give up," the Kid said, and started to slow down his horse.

I don't know what got into me, but it made me mad. "I don't *want* to give up!" I hollered at him, and gave Old Red what he needed, which was a swat on the fanny. "We aren't caught yet! Let's *go!*" That truck had moved right behind us, but instead of shooting at us or telling us we were under arrest, all they did was honk, like they wanted us to get off the road.

"Yer right, Cloudy, son, we got a chance," the old man said, a light in his eye. "Stay right in the center, son. Can't be more'n a quarter of a mile!" He started slapping that horse of his with his hat again and got him into a full gallop. We moved down the road like race horses in the final stretch.

"Move to the side of the road, please. The side of the road." That stone-faced general's voice sounded like it was coming out of a rock, too. "Official business, sir. I command you to move to the side of the road."

"Stay right in the center, Cloudy, that there soldier

boy don't own this here road!" Then he shouted, "There she is, Cloudy! Right over there!"

It was an old sod house, maybe ten yards off the road, and we scooted over there in front of the dust. We hid behind a wall and got off our horses and waited. The army truck marched on through the draw like a tornado, dust billowing up behind; and lagging back so they didn't have to chew the dirt was the posse. "*We* can't get in front of that truck!" one of the men said. They'd slowed down to a trot.

"Can so. We can go right over that hill and come down on top of them. It'd be easy."

"You go ahead, but I'm staying on the road. I'm not riding my horse through some prairie dog town where she'd stick her foot in a hole and break a leg."

"You don't suppose they're over by that old house?" one of them said.

"Naw, we'd've seen 'em." Their voices faded into a blur when they got in front of us, and I peeked around the corner of the house. I watched them ride on up the road, then go around a corner, out of sight.

I turned and looked at the old man, but he had his finger over his lips and otherwise looked like he was fighting off a laughing attack. "What do we do now?" I whispered.

"We tippy-toe out of here like we just stole all the cookies out of the kitchen." He grabbed Old Red by the reins and started to lead him across the road to the hill on the other side. "Don't stir up any dust now, Cloudy, which might could give us away, and keep low; we ain't out of the woods yet. But it looks like we done it, Cloudy son." He patted the gunnysack that was lashed to his saddle. "We robbed that bank, boy, and we got away! Yessir, we got *away!*"

ELEVEN

The prairie between Sheridan and the Big Horns was covered over with sage and brush, with piles of rocks sticking up here and there, and now and then an old cottonwood tree. It got hillier the closer we came to the mountains, and in the draws were old dried-up creek beds. We stayed low as we could, walking our horses around the hills instead of going over the tops, and keeping in the draws, out of sight. There weren't hardly any roads but whenever we'd come to one we'd cross it as fast as we could and keep going. The old man said we couldn't ride on the roads because that's where the posse would be, as soon as the fools who had tried to catch us gave up. He said the rest of them would try to hunt us down without getting out of their cars.

There were a lot of questions I wanted to ask, but I couldn't seem to bring myself to do it. I couldn't make up my mind whether the old man was Tom O'Day or Kid Curry. Thinking he might be Tom

O'Day tore away all the confidence in him I'd had. It came to me kind of hard that I was an outlaw now, on the lam for having robbed a bank. I wanted my partner to be someone I could depend on. Still, Miss Landusky said that Tom's "schemes" never worked, and we'd robbed the bank and were five miles out of town and had even given the posse the slip. So I couldn't decide.

We plugged along on a game trail below the ridge between Soldier Creek and Big Goose. Now and then our horses would step over a gopher hole or push through some bushes with little crinkly green leaves that looked dry enough to burn. Once in a while we'd see a pile of dust rise up out on the prairie, and we'd get off our horses and find some shallow place to hide until we could find out what it was. The old man would have me crawl through the brush to a high spot where I could see, and mostly it was stock that got stirred up over something or other, or someone driving along a road. Once it was some antelope that either got spooked or was just having a good time.

When it got near supper time it started to cool and the Big Horns stood up so straight they looked like they might fall over on us. I didn't see how we'd ride horses into those mountains, but the old man wasn't worried, and I figured if it didn't bother him, whoever he was, it wasn't going to bother me, either.

"Somethin' eatin' at you, Cloudy?"

"What?"

"You look troubled, son. I've noticed too the way you been lookin' at me. Course I don't expect much, as old as I am, and fat, and ugly as a lizard—and you *listen* as good as you always do, which is whenever you feel like it—but something ain't there now, or maybe it's that something *is* there now that wasn't there before." He sat on Old Red with his hat above his ears, looking soft some way, but worried about how I felt.

"I never robbed a bank before."

"Mmmm. Well now, don't you worry about that. Besides, *you* didn't rob it, *I* did. Now that's a fact, although I have to admit if a judge was to pass on the subject, he'd say we both robbed it. That's the law. Now just explain to me how the law works sometime when you have about a year with nothing else to do. If you can figure it out, you're either a genius or a lawyer or a moron or dead. Here the law is, as full of fine points and exceptions and distinctions as anything, but there you were *outside* the bank and there I was *inside* it, and the law just kind of glosses over all that in some mysterious way and says we both robbed it. I tell you Cloudy . . ."

Then a funny thing happened to the way I felt about him. The more he talked, the more I got so I didn't care whether he was a dangerous outlaw who had killed Pike Landusky and two or three sheriffs and some others, or a harmless one who couldn't do anything right. I was stuck with him whoever he was, for one thing, and for another, I really liked the old geezer. If he wanted to think he was Kid Curry, well, that was all right by me. I just wished I knew though, because one way, he'd be taking care of me, and the other, I'd be watching out for him.

We came around a hill and spotted some wrangler from the PK Ranch down in a meadow below us with a bunch of cows, keeping them company. We skirted about a mile south to stay out of his way. The Kid said we had to get past the little town of Wolf before stopping that night, so I had a hunch we wouldn't get that far. Nothing seemed to turn out exactly the way he planned it out. Maybe he knew what I was thinking because he started in talking about how important it is to set your sights high in life, instead of low. "Course once you get them up there with the stars you might say, you've got to prepare for some disappointments. But the important thing is what it does for you, and what it does is keep you always a-tryin' *hard*. Take my own case as an example. I'd easily have been a millionaire right now, tryin' as hard as I try, except for the longest string of bad luck in America. I've been unlucky for more than sixty years in a row, which is ever since the day I was born. The only lucky thing ever happened to me, near as I can tell, is runnin' into you, Cloudy. A thing like that can change a man's luck, too. Why, I bet if I live to be a hundred, I might have a turn of good luck in there and might could make enough money so I don't have to live in that monkey cage the rest of my life. Must be like livin' in heaven to . . ."

He kept right on talking even though he and his horse nearly disappeared in a marshy place we were crossing to get on the other side of Soldier Creek. He made it across somehow without even getting his feet wet, which made me think his luck was a lot better than he knew. Then we rode to the other side of the stream and started to climb.

Pretty soon we rode into the shadows from the Big Horns and it got cool, although it was still more comfortable for snakes than for humans. We let the horses water, and we took some for ourselves and had a rest. He said we'd gone a lot farther south than we should have, but the mark of success was in knowing how to turn a bad situation into an advantage. All you need is practice, he said, and before long you can turn disaster into benefit. I got myself ready for a snowstorm or something else we hadn't figured on. Then he said that this way we wouldn't have to go through Windy Canyon, which was steep, but could get down in Red Canyon and make a camp in the trees next to the stream. He'd already given up on getting to the town of Wolf, which suited me, because I was awful tired and hungry. So we started down into Red Canyon which was more like a cliff. It was so steep we had to get off and lead our horses down a path about wide enough for a medium-sized squirrel. If Windy Canyon was any steeper, the only way in would have been by parachute.

It was dark when we came to the creek, which made soft gurgle sounds as we got nearer. We couldn't see it in the dark though and the Kid was looking for it when he fell into it. He spoke colorfully for about ten minutes after that, accusing the stream of turning in front of him, but started to laugh after a while and said it felt good and he was glad it happened. It cooled him off, which is what he wanted. The suddenness of it was what had angered him, he said. He'd have preferred some warning. But at least now his horse didn't smell so bad, he said. Neither did he, but I didn't tell him, because I probably was a little gamey smelling too.

We found a clearing and he said we could start a fire because posses didn't ride at night anymore and all the Indians were on the reservation. It got me thinking about Arosho and I told him what Miss Landusky had said about that renegade Indian who had bragged he'd come to the rodeo, and the way she looked funny at that Cheyenne who didn't even look like a Cheyenne, and how I wondered if he was Arosho, even though Miss Landusky said he wasn't. The Kid asked me some questions about just what had happened, and whether the Crows and the Cheyennes were walking near one another, and I told him no, there were some floats in between.

He snorted through his nose and told me to get some wood and not worry about it. For one thing, there wasn't an Indian anywhere in Wyoming that a bullet couldn't get through and he had his pistol and a whole boxful of cartridges somewhere. And for another, Arosho was one of those mangy Crows and the Cheyennes wouldn't have let him walk with them anyway. The last he heard, the Cheyennes and the Crows were still at war.

I was hungry enough to eat the old man's saddle and was sure glad when he got around to fixing us some food. He had a fishhook and some line and told me to string a worm on it and set it somewhere and we'd see about fish for breakfast, and then he dug out some beef jerky and some flour and made us some biscuits. That beef jerky tasted like it was made out of salt, and I had to drink enough water to float a canoe, but it still tasted good.

It didn't seem that the old man stopped talking long enough to eat but he must have because all the food he'd set out was gone in five minutes and hard as I went, he still put away most of it. Even so, he saved the last piece for me and said he was full, so I ate it, and he sighed like a hungry dog when the meat was gone. Then we stretched out on the grass near the fire and I rolled in a blanket and didn't do much more than blink at the stars, and I was asleep.

When I next opened my eyes I thought I was still in a dream, everything was so pretty. The cliff face to the west kind of glowed with a soft pink light and as I watched, the colors got deeper. The rocks were layered on that cliff like a stack of pancakes, some of them red and some of them almost white; and here and there some trees or bushes had wedged into the cracks and ledges between the layers of rock. From where I was they looked like hunks of moss, they were so dark and green.

I felt something nearby, but it didn't seem to matter, like in a dream. I even heard a soft "shh, shh, shh" sound, like a duck might make if it tried to walk on pine needles, but that didn't matter either.

My eyes closed after that, all on their own.

bear had ahold of my arm and gave it a jerk, so I sat up. I had it in mind to give that bear a swat. "Hee hee hee!" the old man went, and the dream I'd been in popped like a bubble of soap. Then he whipped off his hat and smacked me on the head with it and laughed like that was the funniest thing he'd ever done.

It made me mad and I got up and started chasing after that crazy old man. I even picked up a rock and stumbled along behind him. "You can't catch me, Cloudy, I'm too fast!" he hollered—and all at once, he dropped out of sight.

I knew I could catch him all right—when there I was on the edge of the stream and couldn't stop. "Whoa, old hoss!" he yelled and I saw out of the corner of my eye where he'd ducked under the bank, as happy as a clown. I went sprawling off the bank and into the water.

"That's the way, Cloudy, get right up out of bed

and jump in the stream! Never could do it myself but you take the Sundance Kid, now he could do it. In fact I seen him do it once in January, to clear his head of all the whisky he'd had the night before, and if . . . Now Cloudy, you put down that rock."

I was wet as a dishrag and shivering, but I didn't care. I still had that rock in my hand, standing right in the middle of the creek, and I took aim. He stood up then and the look in his eye was very, very serious.

"If you was to throw that rock, Cloudy, and if it was to hit me somewhere, I believe what I'd do is get down in that water where you are and sit on you, and I might let you up for air and I might not." I sloshed on through the stream a little closer. I didn't want to miss. "Now you played a trick on me and I played one on you, son. That makes us even."

"That was two weeks ago. Besides, you told me it rinsed you out." I was so mad I wanted to kill him.

"Now Cloudy, I ain't talkin' about when you floated those thistles by me and I took in a hundred or so because that truly did clean me out, and I thank you for it because I haven't had a flu bug since. There just isn't anything left inside me for them little critters to get a grip on. What I'm talkin' about is this morning, finding all them wet rocks in my boots. I have to admit when I put my foot in there and broke three or four toes, at first I didn't see the humor in it. Not at . . . "

"I didn't put any rocks in your boots."

That stopped him, long enough to change directions.

"Well a' *course* you put rocks in my boots. Now just stand there a minute and think on it, and you'll know you did, even if you don't remember doin' it. First thing, why would *I* put rocks in my boots? I'd have no *reason*. But you'd have a reason, don't you see, which is devilment. We can even take it a step further. If I had put rocks in there, then I'd know about it. And if I knew my boots was full of rocks, would I go ahead and cram my feet in them anyway?" He looked real proud of himself, like he had me in a corner and knew there was no way out.

I lost interest in paying him back, and got out of the stream. It made me feel creepy. "Honest, Kid, I didn't put any rocks in your boots." I remembered that "shh, shh, shh" sound though, which I'd thought was part of a dream, and told him about it. Could it have been Arosho?

He cleared his throat and climbed up on the bank. "Hum!" he said, walking on over to the camp.

I took off my shirt and pants and wrung them out. All that I had on was shorts and tennis shoes and socks, but it was warm in the sun. I stretched my shirt and pants out on a rock to dry, and went over to the camp. "You sure you didn't put any rocks in my boots?"

"I'm positive."

"Hum!" He'd already started a fire, and he tossed in a couple more sticks. "Go see if you caught a fish, will you son?"

"You think he's anywhere he could see us? Maybe we both should go."

"First off, we don't know anything yet. And second, if it was that savage Indian, he could have killed us last night, but he didn't, and they'll never do in the daytime what they can do at night. So go see about them fish."

Everything around our camp was different with the sun on it, and it took me a while to find the line, but there was a fish on it. It wasn't much and it had been chewed on, but I was hungry enough to eat it bones and all. The old man cleaned it and stuck a stick through it and told me to hold it over the fire. I did what he said and in a few minutes I could smell that fish, like chicken boiling in a pot. Then the old man took it off the stick, stripped out the bone, and cut the fish in half. He gave me the big part and I started to put the whole thing in my mouth when he stopped me. "Hold on Cloudy, you can't eat fish like that or you'll catch a bone sidewise in your throat and then what?"

"You took the bones out."

"I see you don't know as much as you might about fish. They have as many bones as the average pine tree has needles, only they ain't anywhere near as obvious about it. The only bones I pulled out of that fish were the ones in plain sight."

I started looking at the thing and sure enough, there

was a whole tangle of little white slivers in there. I started picking them out.

"That ain't gonna do you any good, Cloudy. By the time you get all them bones out you'll be dead of starvation. When it comes to eating fish there is only one way and that is take little bites, like this—" he barely even bit off a corner—"and chew it slow so's you get the bones ground up, and then you can take it down." He gulped, then patted his mouth like a lady at tea, and grinned at me. "See?"

It sure was a lot of work for just a little bit of food but I did it the way he said, and while I was doing it, I figured out why he'd given me the big piece. It must have taken me half an hour just to eat that little bit of fish, and while I was finishing it off, he ate all the apples. Then we rolled up the blankets and tied them onto his saddle, and filled up our canteens and started up the trail.

He said Wolf wasn't even a mile but we could cut over to Wolf Creek from where we were and not go through town, and that the town was so small you could go through it a lot of the time and not even know you'd been there. "You don't miss a thing by not goin' through Wolf, Cloudy. All it has is a school and a church and a jail."

Then he told me how once Butch Cassidy wanted to rob the bank there because it'd be easy to do and easy to get away, and he'd have done it too but there wasn't a bank. "Dangdest place. Nothing in that town you can *steal*. If you was to buy a drink, why you'd have to bring in a chicken or something to pay for it with, and then set it up there on the counter and haggle over the finer points of your bird, and maybe get lucky and she'd lay a egg and you could decide on whether the egg was part of the deal, and then come to an agreement on how much of a bottle a chicken and a egg is worth. Chickens don't bring much in Wolf, though, because there's so many of them. What you need is something rare. Needles and clothespins and coat hangers made out of wire can get you all the chickens you'd ever need, and if Butch had gone in there and cleaned that town out, he'd have come away with needles and clothespins and coat hangers. Don't ever let anybody tell you . . . "

He kept talking but I quit listening and just tagged along behind on Dot. The stream flattened out and we started across, but the horses stood in the middle for a minute, cooling their legs and drinking. Then we picked up a trail on the other side that left the stream and bent to the west, skirting around the mountain we were on. We left the trees too and our horses plodded along nice and easy on a path worn through a wide open slope covered with flowers and bushes and rocks. Down below, not even a mile away, in a grassy place where two streams came together, I could see about five buildings and a church. I figured that was Wolf but never got the chance to ask, and then we came into some timber and the town was gone.

It sure was pretty, trailing through those woods. The pine trees were tall and green and cool with every now and then a clump of aspen, and the breeze would flutter the leaves like poker chips on a string. Every now and then we'd set off a hubbub of chickadees and robins and squirrels, and once we heard a crashing sound which the Kid said was probably a deer we'd spooked, even though there weren't many left because they'd been pretty well all hunted out. "Used to be food didn't cost anything, that's the way the Indians lived, but what kind of an economy can you have if food is free? Well, I guess it's like most everything, Cloudy, it has good points, and it has bad points.

"But just take and look at it another way. If everything is free then you don't even need banks. Now how could a man with talent like Butch Cassidy get a start in a world that didn't have banks? The only thing them Indians stole off each other was horses, and that don't have anywhere near the excitement of a bank. Now what about that? When you take money from a bank, unless you use dynamite, you have to do like we done and wait until the bank is open, and that means you have to rob it in broad daylight. You can see how that adds flavor to the thing, can't you? Creeping around at night and taking the tether off a bunch of horses—where is the challenge in that? So I say we need banks. Yessir."

I'd never really thought about banks and how come we need them, and the old man's explanation hung together pretty well. Still, it was the kind of thing I'd like to ask my dad about.

Gosh, I thought, feeling kind of lonesome. I wondered if I'd ever see him again.

THIRTEEN

Those horses didn't need to know how to climb ladders, but it would have helped, because when we got to Wolf Creek, the ground just kind of tilted to straight up. The mountain we had to climb stuck up like a wall, with the trail z-ing back and forth between the rocks and brush that hung onto its side. It was real scary, looking down.

But it was pretty, too. Right where we were, nothing much was growing except for grass and flowers and here and there a bush, but on both sides—maybe a hundred yards off—there were tall stands of pine trees and aspen groves. Then there was the sky, just the purest kind of blue, and now and then a hawk would float through the air above us, and he might twitch his wings enough to change his course, or circle over something he'd seen. I wondered how it would feel to float through the air like that and then, for about five seconds, I let myself be a hawk, and I knew.

We gave the horses a rest every mile or so, and the

old man kept looking all around, I guessed for the posse, and after a time the sun quit feeling good on my back and it got hot. I didn't have a hat and the Kid said the rays of the sun, especially at that altitude, would burn off my skin and boil my brains, so he made me put the paper sack the apples had been in on my head. I felt kind of foolish wearing a paper sack, but it didn't bother anybody except me.

Finally we reached a flat place—the Kid called it a "bench"—then turned to the north and started working up Horseshoe Mountain. The sun started in on our other side. The going wasn't near as hard as it had been because the trail wasn't anywhere near as steep. Not long after that, we got off the trail and made one of our own through some low brush. I figured we were getting close—the old man said it was only about a mile—and when we got up on a ridge and looked back, it felt like you could see the whole world. It was easy after that. We were all done climbing. The only hard part was to keep from gawking to where you'd fall off your horse.

The prairie to the north and east was spread below us like a rug that was alive. Mostly it was brown, but it had long streaks of green where the rivers flowed. The old man said we were five thousand feet above it, and I had to look at Dot's legs now and then to make sure they were on the ground, instead of floating, which is what it felt like. Here and there on the prairie there'd be a square patch—a farmer who'd planted something in rows—and behind us, a long ways off but still looking somehow like you could hit it with a rock, was Sheridan.

Then all of a sudden, right below us, were the strangest looking boulders I'd ever seen. They were great big blocks, as big as buildings, all squared off and with sides as smooth as crystal. It looked like they'd been rolling down the steep mountainside when they'd frozen against it and couldn't move. "That's Fallen City down there," the old man said. "Sure is strange, ain't it? Why if it had a fountain or two, like over at Yellowstone, wouldn't surprise me none if the govinment built a road up in here so people could see it, like they done over there. Yessir, that's what we pay taxes for, those that pay. . . ."

"Is that where our hideout is?"

"Nope. Couldn't make a camp down there unless you was a insect and didn't mind living sideways. All our gear is stashed over yonder, in those trees." He pointed ahead maybe three hundred yards to where some trees cropped over the top of another ridge like ivy growing up a wall. We rode toward them.

The sun was still high, but for some reason, those woods started looking awful dark. It felt like those trees had eyes—there was something spooky looking about them—and when we got in amongst them, they seemed to shut behind us like a closet door. "How much farther?" I whispered.

You'd have thought I'd stuck a gun in his back.

"Dang!" he yipped, stiff all over, like his thumb had got caught in a light bulb socket and someone threw the switch. "What was that?" He was whispering, too.

"Me. I just asked how much farther."

"I ain't sure," he said, keeping his voice real low. "It's around here someplace."

"Did you hide it?"

"Course I hid it," he snapped, but still in a whisper. "What if some hunter was to go through here, or some Indian was to sneak off the reservation, just as an example? Now the chances are a thousand to one against anything like that, but you got to plan for the contingencies. But the contingency I didn't plan on was forgetting where I *put* the staggerack." I started to laugh. "Now Cloudy, it don't help none for you to start giggling like that. I need to concentrate on just where the mumblewhumper is, and I concentrate best when it's quiet."

Something got into me. "*QUIET!*"

The old man's red horse started to skip around and even Dot was surprised. "Hee hee hee," the old man went. "I tell you Cloudy, there's something different about you. That cowboy I named you after might take it into his head about once a year to let out a yelp, and he'd have done it just the same way, when nobody was expecting it but it still fit right into the conversation."

It sort of broke the ice, and we stopped whispering.

The woods all around us even looked more friendly, so I was glad I'd done it.

He remembered putting the bedding and clothes in a small cave, inside a pile of rocks, and covering them over with boughs off a fir tree. Then he'd hung the food as high as he could reach in the same tree. The boughs would still be green, he said, so we tethered the horses in a clearing where there was some grass and we split up and started looking.

We hunted around in those woods about an hour and got to know them pretty good. The old man talked a stream the whole time and I was still nervous about something, so I stayed close enough to hear him. I noticed a pile of boulders about twenty feet high that he kept coming back to. Then out in the forest, maybe fifty feet from those rocks, I found a branch off a fir tree. The end looked like it had been snapped off. "Tom?"

He didn't notice I'd called him "Tom" and for a minute, neither did I. "What?"

"Look at this." I came over beside him and showed him the branch.

"Where'd you find that?"

"Over there."

His hand went down on his gun again and his eyes swelled up like they were balloons. Then he skedaddled over to the rocks, and recognized a little cave on the other side. "*That's* why we're a-havin' this trouble," he said. "Somebody went and stole all our gear!"

FOURTEEN

That old man and I stared at each other. "Golly," I said. "Who'd want to do that?"

He sat down on a rock, pulled out his pistol, and broke it open. Then he reached in his pocket and plugged in some bullets. "That whumple Jehosophas savage, that's who. He's playin' with us. If I get half a chance, I'm gonna put a hole in that noble red man as big as a window."

"*Playing* with us!"

"Yup, they do that sometimes. The meat tastes better if you can get the blood goin' through it first."

I didn't know what he was talking about. "What?"

"It's Arosho. It's that renegade Indian friend of Lavonica's. *He's* the one put them rocks in my boots and caused me to sprain my toes. We got *him* to thank for that excitement. He's a-workin' on us now too, tryin' to put us into the proper frame of mind you might say. Then he prob'ly figures to do us like he done that family. Only . . ."

"You mean he's out to kill us?"

The old man's eyes got wide and he swallowed something that went down hard. "Dang, that's what I mean all right. It hadn't really come in on me though until just now." He closed his gun and put it in his holster.

"Why didn't he do it when we were asleep?"

"I told you. It's a game, or more like a ceremony to a Indian. They like to test the mettle of their enemies, so's they can make up a song about it afterwards and sing about it to the whole village. It's what they do for entertainment." He sounded scared and got up, looking every which way. "Now you got to hush up Cloudy, so's I can think. This ain't at all like gettin' chased by that sheriff's posse. I'd rather have *ten* posses after me than one Indian with the blood lust. An Indian like that ain't predictable. He don't even care whether he lives or dies, which ain't natural. He might push a rock on us, or shoot us with a cannon, you can't tell. I got to . . ."

"Shoot us with a cannon?"

"Cloudy, I got to *think*. No, it ain't likely he'd shoot us with a cannon because it'd be terrible hard to bring one up that trail. I can toss that one. Oh, what I wouldn't give for Butch. He'd come up with a plan in a second that'd . . ."

My gosh, I thought, and it made me mad. He

sounded like he really thought Arosho might shoot us with a cannon. I lost the last bit of confidence in him I'd had, and at the same time it scared me, too. "You aren't Kid Curry. You're Tom O'Day!"

He looked like I'd hit him in the stomach with a hammer. He couldn't get his breath. Finally: "Lavonica see me?"

"Yes."

Then his eyes got brittle in some way I didn't like. "Well, I may have been Tom O'Day once, but I ain't that worthless little runt anymore. No sir, I'm Kid Curry now, just the same as you!"

"What?"

"I've changed, don't you see? Same as you did, from Little Lord Fauntleroy Penrose III into a tough little waddie name of Cloudy!"

Brother, I thought. I am in real trouble now. The old man has gone clear around the bend. But I didn't want to make him any crazier than he was, so as far as I was concerned, he was the Kid.

"I got an idea, Kid. Let's give him the money and beat it on out of here."

"What money? Oh, you mean . . . Well, I don't know about that."

The way he said that made me want to see it. "There's a whole gunnysack full of money on your horse," I said. "I'll go get it."

"Wait." He kind of turned his face so I couldn't see

it. "Must have slipped my mind, Cloudy, or I'd have told you. It ain't there now."

"Huh? Where is it?"

He was kicking at a rock, the way I do sometimes when I'm working on an explanation. "I hid it."

I forgot all about him being crazy, and started in thinking maybe he'd hid it so he could grab the money when I was asleep, and run off by himself, and disappear. "Partners, huh?" I jeered at him.

"Hold on, Cloudy, it ain't what you think."

"Well, go ahead then. Tell me another lie."

"This ain't no lie, son," he said, but his eyes didn't look right. "I hid it this morning while you was pullin' in that fish. I got to thinking about them rocks in my boots and figured if you didn't put them in there, maybe somebody else did. I was gonna tell you about it, honest I was, son. Fact is I thought maybe in a week or two you could go back and get it."

"If you were gonna tell me, how come you didn't?"

"I'm tellin' you now, ain't I? Besides, maybe I didn't want to scare you. Now it's different though. Now it looks like both of us just plain got to be scared."

I didn't know whether to believe him or not. He hadn't even told the truth about who he was. Besides, he looked at me like he couldn't possibly be lying, which is always what you do when you're right in the middle of one. "We could set a trap," I said.

"What?"

"We could set a trap for that old Indian. I saw in a movie once where . . ."

"A trap! Yessir! Cloudy, all you need is the experience because you *got* the imagination!" He came back to life and the sag went out of him. His eyes even lost that hollow look and picked up some fire. "A little bait and enough line and I bet you we could hook him good! We could . . . oh." The light in his eyes went out. "How we gonna build a trap when he's watching us? You can bet your saddle he's a-watchin' us right now. . . ."

When he said that, it started me to looking all around. "How could he do that and us not know?"

"Easy, for a Indian who's grow'd up without any education and never has lived in a house. Just as easy as for you to read a book. Them Crows is about one half mountain sheep, and the other half is pine tree. You can look right at 'em and not even see 'em because they'll turn theirselves into a rock, and then if you *do* notice them, off they'll go through the timber quick as a deer. Let's just stop now a minute and don't even think, and see if you can feel him. I heard where you can tell that way, but it don't work for me. Seems like when I have to, I can't stop and make myself feel nothing, which you have to be able to do. The more I try to feel nothing, the more things start a-goin' through my mind. That's always the way it's been with me, even though . . ."

"He's watching us," I said. "I can feel him."

The old man sagged. "You certain, Cloudy? I mean, do you feel it or do you just think you do, after what I said?"

"He's watching us and kind of laughing."

"Laughing!" The old man started to bristle. "Why, that staggerack! That ignorant no account whumple-dumber! Now listen to me, Cloudy, I got an idea. In about a minute I'm gonna pull out my gun and start shootin' into that juniper bush over there. When I do that you yell at me like you don't like it, like you maybe think that juniper bush is your brother or something, and pick up this big rock and bust me on the head with it. You got to be a little careful about that part. I don't mind a little bruise—I reckon when you're in a tight spot a little bruise won't be such a bad price to pay to get out of it—but what I don't want is a concussion."

Oh man, I thought, the Kid is off his rocker. "Why do that? You'll just . . ."

"When I'm down he'll go for me because he'll want the gun. Then I want you to make a run for that horse of yours and ride about a mile, till the trail gets steep. Wait for me there. You got that now? All right, Cloudy, here we . . ."

"Hey, *wait*." I was really scared. He had his pistol out and all I could think was what Miss Landusky said, about how none of Tom O'Day's schemes ever worked. "Kid, what if . . ."

"I'm thinkin' of the way it'll look, boy. He'll think you and me had an argument and you conked me on the head and ran. He'll come after me first because I'm down and have the gun, and when he does—zing! I got him! Some things you can't ponder over or take a vote on, Cloudy. Some things you just got to *do!*"

"But . . ."

"No buts! Yah-hoo! This is *me*, boy, the real article! I'm Kid Curry, just bustin' for a fight!" He had his gun out and blared a shot into the juniper bush. "*Now*, Cloudy, don't wait! Do it *now* while my courage is up!"

I was scared. What if the plan didn't work? But it felt like I had to do something so I picked up the rock, which was so big I could hardly lift it, and lunged forward and dropped it on that crazy old man's shoulder, near his ear. "Ai-ai-ai!" he yipped, and fell like a log. I thought for sure he was dead. But he looked up at me from the ground out of one eye. *"Git,"* he whispered, and I started running.

I got to the clearing where the horses were tethered, going full steam, and Dot looked at me with a mouthful of grass. That crazy old fool, I thought to myself. He doesn't know what he's doing and Arosho'll kill him and it's all my fault for thinking his plan might work. Dot looked up at me, wondering about all the excitement. . . .

And then I saw him. He was the same Indian Miss Landusky had sucked in her breath at, and he just kind of grew out of the ground between me and Dot. When I realized where he was, I tried to run.

"Kid! *Kid!* He's over—" A hand closed over my mouth.

Then I don't know what happened, but it felt like I was falling off a bridge.

FIFTEEN

The next thing I remember, it was night, and the stars were like white sparks in the sky. There was a big old moon behind a tree, and the moonlight made everything look like different shades of blue, except for the shadows. The shadows in the forest had been turned into black holes of nothing.

I was cold and shivery, and when I tried to move, I found out my hands were tied behind my back. I could move my feet though, and could even get up. I started out of there on the run, but after ten feet I got jerked to the ground. I'd been tethered like a horse to a tall aspen tree, as big around as a fence post.

There was no sign of Arosho or the old man, and everything I could see was still as death. I wished I'd never seen that stupid bank. "Kid! Hey, *Kid!*"

That yelling really scared me at first, because I didn't know who'd go around hollering like that. Then I found out it was me.

It was too cold to sleep, and the ground felt wet, so

I started in walking around that old aspen tree. I didn't know what to do. My eyes and cheeks kind of itched and I could taste some salt. Had I been crying? Man oh man, I thought, wondering about it. Robbing a bank can sure get complicated.

I tried to untie the rope around my wrists with my fingers, but they wouldn't reach to the knots. Then I thought I could at least take the tether off. But the rope was looped around the tree over a branch about seven feet off the ground, and I couldn't reach that, either.

I sure could have used a drink of water. My lips felt like two pieces of bark. Then I started in feeling hungry and a big wad of saliva worked into my mouth and that helped a little. I rinsed it around sort of and worked the dryness out of my throat. The trouble was, it got me thinking about food.

Not for long, though. I could hear something moving—kind of a rustle—like a herd of snakes on the march. That put my hair out and really bristled my skin. Then the sound stopped, and then a little later it picked up but moved away. I started in hearing all kinds of sounds after that. Mostly they were just crickets or hoot owls, but sometimes there'd be a scritch or a whisper that'd lift my eyes and ears about an inch away from my head.

Was I going to die? I wondered. Would Arosho really kill me?

It felt like a year later when the sky in the east

started to lighten and slowly the stars winked out. There wasn't anything to do but watch, and another time it might have been fun. Then all of a sudden, I realized how pretty it was. The trees in the morning light looked like something I'd never seen before. At first they were just blobs the shape of bruises, but after a while they turned into drawings, and later they picked up color and filled out.

I'd come to know the ring around that aspen tree pretty well, but still it was different by the time the sun got to it. The thing I'd been tripping on in the dark was a stump instead of a rock, and the squishy thing I'd walked through was an anthill. Those ants didn't like it, either. They had worked off the sharp edges that my feet had cut in their hill, but it seemed to me like they were looking for enemies.

I thought about hopping around in it like I did to the anthills in the vacant lot next to my house in Denver. The ants would really get excited and roam around afterwards, looking for something to bite. I'd never felt a bit sorry for any of them, either, but would stomp on every one I could see, like it was a war.

I decided not to do that this time. I was tied to that tree and couldn't get away, and that's no time to start a fight with a million ants.

I tried to make myself still the way the old man said, and feel whether Arosho was watching me—but after a while it got so I couldn't tell. There were too many things on my mind. Why did he want to kill me? I wondered. What did I ever do to him?

What I wished was that he'd bring me a bowl of ice cream first. My throat was really dry. It got so I couldn't even swallow. Then I decided as long as he was going to kill me anyway it didn't matter if I poisoned myself to death, so I bit off an aspen leaf and chewed it up.

That got some juices working in my mouth, and I swallowed it. I'd tasted aspen leaves before and knew what to expect—sour as a lemon almost, and they'll draw your cheeks together like they are being sewed— but just then, it tasted pretty good. Sometimes when I'm miserable it doesn't take much to make me laugh, and I don't know why but I started laughing. Chewing on those leaves and liking how they tasted struck me as funny. Maybe I *am* different, I thought. Then I got down on my knees and started to examine the grass. Maybe I could just graze along like Dot for food, and wait for it to rain for water, and then go galloping off if I had the chance. There were some sweet peas in bloom and some dandelions and I ate them and waited to die, but nothing bad happened except my teeth felt green. I even tried some grass, but didn't like it because it was too stringy.

By that time it was already hot. I wasn't anywhere near satisfied, but decided to stop grazing anyway. I moved as far from that anthill as I could and laid down on my side in the shade. It wasn't comfortable at all.

My hands were tied behind my back, so I had to stretch out on my stomach, which put all that grass in my face. I tried the other side but still couldn't get my head feeling right. It hung toward the ground and made my neck sore. I worked my shoulder into the dirt and kind of leaned toward my back, which wasn't too bad. In fact I must have gone to sleep because the next thing I knew, it was raining and I was cold again.

That water sure tasted good! I got up and turned my face right into the rain, and shut my eyes and opened my mouth, and worked my tongue all around. I'd never known how rain can taste so fine. But trying to drink it was like grazing in a way, and it came to me why every time you see a cow, her nose is in the grass. It doesn't matter how long you spend at it, you just can't seem to get enough. I tried to let as much rain fall in my mouth as would go in, and when it stopped raining, I licked as many drops off the aspen leaves and grass as I could. But it seemed like all I did was get my tongue wet.

Things sure had gotten themselves switched around, I thought. Here the old man had figured out a way to bait a trap to catch Arosho, but now Arosho had turned it upside down. He had me staked out like a bleating lamb, and *I* was the trap, and all Arosho had to do was wait until the Kid tried to cut me loose . . .

If the old man even tried. The way his plans always turned up one or two "contingencies," maybe I'd be better off if he didn't. He was probably on his way back to Red Canyon where he'd hidden the money anyway, and it wouldn't take him long after that to get to a railroad track, and hop on a freight and go to California. . . .

Unless Arosho knew the old man better than I did. I wished my mind would give my head a rest. Miss Landusky had said that old Indian chief knew all about me, just by looking. Could Arosho tell all about Tom?

I tested the rope around my hands and could feel it getting tighter every time I tried to loosen it. I wasn't going anywhere. My only chance was for the old man to take the bait, which meant I hadn't hardly any chance at all. Even if he wanted to help, he'd probably lose his nerve along the way, or else keep it just barely long enough to get both of us killed.

Then after a while I didn't seem to care. My eyes got blurry and my cheeks felt wet which made me think I might be crying, but I didn't care about that, either. I sat down on the ground, as wet as it was, and leaned against that old aspen tree. I wondered how long Arosho would wait. . . .

SIXTEEN

That night it got so cold I could see my breath, and the next day, instead of raining, it hailed. That aspen tree leaked, too, and I huddled under it and shivered, and had the most awful lonely feeling in the world.

"Arosho! Why don't you kill me and get it over?"

I knew who it was who said that: it was me. I was so miserable I wished I could die. My head felt dizzy and the longer I sat there shivering to death, the worse it got. I was shaking so bad I thought the tree would come out by its roots, when things started to slip away from me in the strangest way. First the cold feeling left and everything got still, and it felt like I was falling off a cloud. Then somehow I was drifting over Denver, and settled down real slow in the vacant lot behind my house.

It didn't surprise me at all to be there. It was three years ago when I was nine, and I was whistling a tune and scattering grasshoppers as I cut for the stable where my father kept the horses. The grasshoppers'd jump up and go "whirrrrrrr!"—all steamed up over being disturbed—and fly out in an arc. Then they'd land on the ground or a weed and wait for another insult.

This wasn't like any dream I'd ever had, where anything goes, and you don't know what to expect. Everything in this one was real, like it was really happening. I could feel the sun on my back and dirt under my feet, and when I looked off toward the mountains west of Denver, I saw the same high, white clouds. I picked up a rock and zunked it toward the gopher hole by the gate—not trying to hit anything, just trying to keep that old gopher from getting fat—then climbed over the railing by the stable and went in.

My pony was sure glad to see me. He was a Shetland but colored like a palomino; my father used to say from a distance people thought he was a Saint Bernard. He even named the horse "Fido" and bought him a dog collar. My dad was just being funny in that way of his, and it made my mother laugh. But he was as serious as a preacher when he told me to put the collar on the horse, and I couldn't tell whether he was being funny or not.

Fido showed me his teeth in a grin, then raised some dust with his right front hoof as he scratched the dirt. Then he leaned back and swished his tail around and started to step in a circle to the left. That meant he wanted to go for a ride. He'd always move around like that when I went to put on the saddle, just to keep me on my toes and see if I'd get it on his back or miss him and plop it on the ground.

I got it on, though, and cinched it up, and I could see the veins in his belly kind of swell and deflate, so I loosened it some and scratched his chest where I knew it itched. I got the bit in his mouth and led him out into the yard, then mounted him and started down the gravelled driveway for the street.

"Where are you going, dear?" my mother asked. She was sitting on the sun porch, reading a book.

"I don't know," I said, remembering how pretty and nice she was.

"Well, I certainly hope you don't get lost."

That was kind of a funny thing to say, and I laughed.

"Would you mind running an errand for me on your way?"

"No'm, I wouldn't mind."

She got up too fast, and had to steady herself. She was real sick then but didn't know it. "Mrs. Player is not feeling very well, dear. I baked her some cookies. You must promise me you won't eat any of them."

"I promise."

Mrs. Player lived all by herself in a little house on Syracuse Street, and it would give me somewhere to go. I got up on Fido while she went in to get the cookies, and while I waited, I nailed a mosquito in the act.

I knew it would itch, and it did. Sometimes I'll let

134

them get part of a load anyway, because they are easier to hit while feeding.

"Be careful, dear," Mom said, handing me the cookies. "I don't want you to get run over crossing Quebec. And I particularly don't want Mrs. Player to get a box of crumbs."

I could always tell when my mom was teasing. She smiled at me in a way that made me feel good, and squeezed my hand. " 'Bye, Mom," I said.

Then as I rode across the vacant lot toward Quebec Street, I got to wondering how she'd feel if she knew I'd robbed a bank, but something was wrong, because I hadn't robbed one yet. . . .

"Cloudy."

That surprised me, because that isn't the way it had happened, either. I looked around from up on top of Fido, trying to see who'd said that.

"Cloudy!"

There it was again. It was just a whisper, but it went through me like snow down my neck. I'd been holding the reins with one hand and rattling the box of cookies up next to my ear with the other. . . .

"Be . . . real . . . quiet."

Everything started to fade. I didn't want to leave; because it was warm there in Denver, and I knew when I got to Mrs. Player's, she'd give me some cookies from the box, and a glass of milk.

"Roll . . . toward . . . me . . . nice . . . and . . . slow."

I opened my eyes and it was so dark I couldn't see

anything. There weren't any stars or moon: rain sleeted through me, powered by a wind that crashed around in the trees like an angry ghost: my teeth were chattering and my whole body was shaking, and I was never so miserable in my life.

"Kid?"

"Shhhh." The sound came from right in front of me and then I saw a shape next to me that was darker than everything else. It was the Kid! That crazy old man hadn't left for California after all!

I rolled like I was rolling in my sleep and put my back next to him where he could reach my hands. He whispered in my ear while he cut me loose. He said Arosho had scattered the horses and would come after us if we tried to run, so we needed a plan. I wanted to leave without a plan, but didn't say so. He told me to stay where I was for the rest of the night, and pretend I was still tied up, and then in the morning, when there was plenty of light, get up and run toward Fallen City. The Kid said he would hide at the other end of the clearing we were in. Arosho would think I'd worked myself free, and when he came after me, the Kid would bring him down.

I wanted to get up and start running right away, and told him so. Look at the way his other plan had worked. But the old man said we couldn't go anywhere that night anyway because you couldn't see your hand in front of your face. But even though *we* couldn't see in the dark, that no-account Indian probably could, because that's the way they are raised. He also said that this was a plan that couldn't miss, and even Butch would like. And another thing. After he'd put a hole in that savage, then I could go find the horses, which he needed because he was too old to walk. So he cut the rope off my hands and told me I had to keep my hands like they were, then smooth as a worm, he disappeared.

If he'd really been Kid Curry, it wouldn't have been so hard for me just to wait. But he was Tom O'Day, a worthless outlaw, and sure as anything, something would go wrong. I was about frozen, too, and it sure was a tempation to use my hands. Still, I stuck them behind me, like he said.

Then for some reason my teeth quit their clicking and my body started to get warm. That grass began to feel like a pillow and the next thing I knew, I was asleep.

SEVENTEEN

When I woke up the sun was warming my face and my hands were cradled under my cheek. I didn't think anything about it, it felt so good just to lie there nice and comfortable—when I realized where my hands were. I almost sat up and snapped them behind my back, but Arosho was probably watching and he'd see me do that, so I stayed the way I was and tried to think what to do.

My mind wouldn't work the way I wanted it to. Maybe it was all tired out, because instead of concentrating on the problem, it started noticing how pretty and clean everything was. Little drops of water had gathered on the grass and flowers and hung from the needles of the trees, and now and then in the sunlight, they'd flicker blue. The bark on the aspen was so clean and white it shined like my mother's teeth. I just let my eyes relax and saw the gnats and butterflies draw lines in the air, like running your finger through water, where the line will stay for a second and then disappear.

I couldn't think what to do. There was plenty of light and maybe I should get up and start running, like the Kid had planned. The trouble was if Arosho had seen my hands weren't tied, he'd know it was a trap. I sure wished I knew where he was—and then something in me got tight and prickly, the way you get when you know someone's behind you, ready to scare you.

I heard a sound—a tree branch swishing, only there wasn't any wind—and rolled toward my other shoulder to see what it was.

I saw Arosho! He'd dropped out of a tree across the clearing—the branch quit moving—he was still as a rock and if I hadn't known he was there, I'd have missed him. I half closed my eyes to make him think I hadn't seen him, but I don't think it fooled him any. He didn't move. He seemed rooted to the ground in the shadows, like a tree stump, and then I knew the old man was back in there somewhere, too!

Suddenly it came to me what was going on. Arosho knew where the old man was hiding, and was after him. I had to warn the old man! Without even thinking I got up and started to sing, like I was crazy. It was kind of a chant, like I was an Indian and the forest needed rain. "Hey hey hey hey Kid Kid Kid Kid by by the the tree tree tree tree Indian by the tree tree tree tree he he sees sees . . ."

The old man jumped up! He'd been in a juniper bush about thirty feet from Arosho and there he was, looking at the wrong tree! "*Which one!*" he yelled. "*Which one!*"

Arosho ran in a way I'd never seen. He was like a bullet that had only one thing to do, which was hit the target. "Behind you!" I hollered, watching it happen and not able to stop any of it.

By the time the Kid got turned around, Arosho was on him! I saw a knife in Arosho's hand reach out like the tongue of a snake and flick at the old man, touching him twice, and then the gun went off. Arosho jerked. Then that brown arm went up high and came down hard on the lump of blue that was the Kid. He staggered and the gun dropped out of his hand. The Indian, all bent over, watched him go down.

Arosho turned and looked at me, holding his stomach with one hand and the knife in the other. He had sagged like he might crumple to the ground, but caught himself before falling down. Slowly he moved the hand that had been over his stomach—it was covered with blood—and made a motion with it that I'd seen before. It was the same sign he'd given to Miss Landusky at the parade! Why? I wondered, hating him for what he had done. He stumbled off into the trees, and I was glad the Kid had shot him.

I ran over to the juniper bush where the old man was. He was on his hands and knees, and he looked like a dog that was throwing up. There were splotches of blood that kept growing in his clothes, and I had the awful feeling he was going to die. All I could do was get my arms around that crazy old man, and pat him, and cry.

But he was laughing! "I *done* it, Cloudy, just like I said! I put a bullet right . . . in . . . his . . . gut!" He coughed and breathed hard, like the only way to get any air was to suck it through cotton, then he flopped over on his back. Somehow his head got stuck on my leg.

I didn't want him to die. He was my partner; we'd robbed a bank together. "Come on, Kid, just wait while I get some water, and you'll be all right, you'll see!" I was blubbering like a fool, and couldn't seem to let go of his neck.

"Cloudy, it don't matter." His voice was the softest kind of whisper and sounded peaceful, like the smile on his face. "I'm an old man, son, and them cuts don't hurt. Fact is, I can't even feel 'em. But you know what I feel?"

"No, Kid, don't!"

He kind of patted me. "Listen to me, son, I got to tell you. I feel brave!" I could see some blood in his mouth, but it didn't seem to bother the old man. "Here I been tryin' all my life to be brave, but the harder I'd try, the more foolish would be the thing I done. But today, I *done* it!" His eyes kind of lost their focus. He coughed, and some blood spilled over his chin, and I wanted to get something to wipe it off with but couldn't leave. "I'm proud, Cloudy," I heard him say. "For the first time in my life. I'm proud."

Then the old man died.

After a while I was able to move. All our bedding and extra clothes were stacked up under a tree, and the food was tied up in the same tree. I got it down and ate a little, then put some oats in a pan and rattled them around so the horses would hear them—and got the scare of my life.

There was Arosho, sitting on the ground with his back against a tree, staring at me. It scared me so bad I couldn't move. I was just standing there, waiting for him to get up off the ground and come kill me, when I noticed that some flies were working around his eyes, but he didn't blink.

My gosh, I thought to myself. He's dead, too.

I started to shake, which is what I'd been doing before with the oats in the pan. I had the strangest urge, too, to go get the Kid's gun and empty it into Arosho's body. "Murderer," I said, staring at his dead eyes and hating him. I didn't care what Miss Landusky thought. He was a murdering savage, and I was glad he was dead.

There was a rustle in the bushes that froze me over again, but it was Dot. She must have heard the oats rattling in the pan. "Hey, Dot, come here, Dot. Boy am I glad to see you!" She came up to me and put her nose under my cheek, and gave me a kind of big old wet horse kiss. It sure felt good. I patted her and hugged her and she must have thought I was crazy, but she didn't care. She just dug into the oats.

It was really hard for me to move after that. I felt like somebody had pulled a plug in my body and drained out all the oil. I guess I was just plain tired, but knowing what was wrong didn't make it any easier. It took a while to find that old red horse of the Kid's, but I finally got both horses tethered and then made the old man as comfortable as I could make him. His gun was next to his side, and I took it and broke it open, and saw there were four bullets in the cylinder. I closed it and stuck it in my belt. Then I wrapped him up in a blanket as tight as I could so the ants would have to work harder to get at him. I even went back across the clearing to where Arosho was and did the same for him, although I wasn't anywhere near as gentle about it. His eyes kept looking at me, like there was something more he wanted me to do. I closed them up, and instead of taking his knife, I put it next to him before wrapping him up.

There was a lot that needed to be done, but I couldn't make myself do any of it. After a while I got out another blanket and rolled up in it to take a short nap. I took the pistol out and put it by my head, then lay there feeling nice and warm in the sun. The nap took longer than I thought. When I woke up the stars were so bright they looked like holes in the night, and I was wrapped up and warm as a piece of toast.

I knew where I was, too, and what had happened, and I felt bad when I thought about it. There was nothing to do in the night, though, so I went back to sleep.

It didn't last long. I woke sitting straight up, ready to run. The sky had started to lighten, and I could see my breath. But the shrieks and screams were what had my attention. It was awful. "Coyotes!" I said to myself, which I'd heard before, but never so close. It sounded like a hundred cats being electrocuted.

The Kid? I thought, jumping up and searching around for that pistol of his. But he wasn't the one they were fighting over. I could see his body fifty feet away, covered and still. They'd started in on Arosho.

I yelled as loud as I could, and ran right at them. "Get out of here! Get! Get away!" I hollered, mad as could be. I didn't want them chewing up on Arosho, even if he had wanted to kill me.

It took those coyotes by surprise. They gave off a few yips and a couple of snarls and backed away, but not very far. So I shot at one of them, and the explosion took me by surprise. It practically blew off my ears, and the gun jumped out of my hand and lit on the ground. The coyotes ran away. They'd gotten the blanket off him, but hadn't done much more than take a hunk out of his leg.

I found the blanket and rolled him up in it again, then started dragging him over by the Kid. It was all the way across the clearing, about two hundred yards, and by the time I got him there the sun was up.

Varmints had found the food, which was my fault for leaving it all over the place, instead of tying it up and hanging it from the tree. But I found some cheese that smelled so bad the varmints wouldn't eat it, and some peanut butter in a jar, and some bread. It was delicious. I sat there on a tree stump enjoying breakfast, when I looked up and saw a couple of buzzards circling in the sky. It gave me the creeps.

I had to figure out a way to get the Kid and Arosho down to Sheridan. I wasn't going to leave either one of them for the buzzards, or the coyotes, or the bugs. It meant I'd have to turn myself in, and the Kid had said bank robbers usually get about twenty years, and I sure didn't want to spend twenty years behind bars. But I couldn't see any way out of it. Besides, I was only twelve and small for my age, and I thought maybe the judge would take pity on me. I might even be out of prison in time for college.

I decided the best way to get them down was to build a travois out of blankets and poles. About five of those big, black buzzards were up there now, looking things over, and I wondered if they were getting ready to attack. I got me a club and some rocks to fight them off with, just in case. I'd stuck the Kid's gun back in my belt, but my ears were still kind of vibrating, and I didn't want to have to shoot it again. I started walking over to the aspen grove looking for poles—but I stopped dead in my tracks. There was a man in there, on horseback, staring at me.

It scared me as bad as the day before, when I'd found Arosho. Except this time, there weren't any flies around the man's eyes. He was a big man who wore glasses that he had to squint through. "Ain't you Alex Penrose?" he asked, his voice in kind of a whisper.

"Yes sir," I said. He had his gun out and I put up my hands, realizing I'd been caught. They probably had a poster out on me, and I wondered how big the reward was for my capture.

"Well, I declare. Come over here, son," he said, motioning and still keeping his voice low. "What are you doing up in these mountains? We thought that kidnapper'd taken you to Denver!"

"What?"

"Got to keep your voice down, son. There's an Indian up here somewhere who's gone bad."

"Arosho?"

"That's the one! A Crow! You seen him?"

"Yes sir, he's right over there," I said, pointing. "He's dead."

"Dead! You sure about that?" He noticed the gun in my belt. "Did you kill him?"

"No sir it wasn't me. It was . . ." But then I didn't know what to say. His real name was Tom O'Day, but to me, he was the Kid.

"That feller who kidnapped you? Say. Where's he at?"

"He's over there too."

The man squinted his eyes at me. "Well, you mean he's dead?"

"Yes sir."

He pushed his hat back with the barrel of his gun, and relaxed. "There anybody else up here who's dead? Looks to me like you cleaned up on the whole lot of them."

"No sir, I didn't do anything," I said, trying to figure out what he was talking about. Why did he think I'd been kidnapped?

"We knew somebody was dead," the man said. "Look at all them buzzards. We thought that wild Indian had killed some more folks." He poked his arm in the air and fired off two shots. "Wait'll the sheriff hears about this!"

When he said "sheriff," my stomach got that real hollow feeling it gets when you know you're caught. "Am I under arrest?" I asked.

"You! Under arrest! What for?" he asked, steadying his horse after the shots.

"Well, for . . . Because . . ."

"You was kidnapped, son. By that feller Tom O'Day, or Kid Curry, or whoever he was. Your folks are on their way back from Paris, France, this very moment, with the ransom money." He leaned down and reached for my arm. "Ain't a crime to get kid-napped. Here! Let's go see them pore dead souls." He swung me up behind him. "A whole posse of us up here lookin' for that wild Indian, some of the best trackers in Wyoming, and you tell me that outlaw's already kilt him!"

My gosh, I thought, trying to take it all in. I was sure glad I was behind him where he couldn't see my face. "Well, didn't I hear the bank in Sheridan was robbed on rodeo day?" I asked.

"Not as I knows of, son, and I reckon I'd know, because I'm Sheriff Buford's deputy and we are the law for the whole county. Hi! Get away, dang buzzards!" he hollered, dragging out his gun again and shooting at a bird that had landed on the ground near the bodies. The bird flapped away, along with another one.

I didn't get it. "Wasn't there a posse?" I asked.

"Posse? What're you talkin' about, son?" He stared down at the bodies of Arosho and the Kid.

"I just heard . . . you know, over by the fairgrounds, some shooting and stuff."

"Oh, that," he said, getting off the horse and helping me down, even though I didn't need any help. "Couple of cowboys took some shots, I heard. Got chased off by some boys whose noses was out of joint." He lifted the blanket from Arosho's face, not paying any atten-tion to me. "That's him all right, by golly! Dead as a doornail!"

Three other men, all on horseback, rode into the

148

clearing from different directions. "Sheriff! The Indian's dead!" the deputy hollered, lowering the blanket. "I bet it was one heckuva fight!"

"Who've you got there, Jed? Who's that boy?" a big man said. He sat on the prettiest black stallion I'd ever seen.

"Oh. This here's Alex Penrose, Sheriff, that boy who was kidnapped."

"You don't say! Well this is some kind of day!" The sheriff jumped off his horse and came over to me and stuck out his hand. He had a badge on his chest and a stomach that hung out over his belt and a huge grin on his face. "Mighty glad to see you, young feller! I'm Sheriff Buford, Clifford Buford, and me and my boys have been out searching for you, too!"

I kind of gulped, and shook his hand.

"Did you kill the Indian? We found out he was at the rodeo, just like he'd said he would be, disguised as a Cheyenne! We been huntin' for him since. Then when we saw all them buzzards circling around, we thought maybe he'd struck again!" The sheriff went over to where the others had gathered around the bodies. They'd peeled the blankets off both men, and the Kid looked peaceful, like he was asleep. "What happened, son? That there's the feller who kidnapped you, ain't it? You kill him too?"

"No sir, I didn't kill anybody."

"Look at them cuts on the outlaw, Sheriff," one of the others said.

"Yeah, but look at the Indian. That kidnapper must have been one tough hombre. Look where he bit that Indian on the leg!"

"Must have been one heckuva fight, all right," Jed the deputy said. "How 'bout it, Alex?"

I nodded my head. My eyes were kind of wet, and I didn't want to say anything very much. "It sure was."

Having all that help made it easy to get Tom and Arosho out of the mountains. They rolled them up in blankets and slung them across Old Red. Then they packed all the gear on Dot, and I rode behind Deputy Jed, and we started down.

It was easy for me to keep quiet because they were deciding what had happened to me, just like my dad does, whether it happened or not. Besides, I'd "been through the wringer," so they left me alone. About the only thing they were interested in anyway was the fight, and I told them how Arosho had snuck up on the Kid and stabbed him, and the Kid had shot Arosho in the stomach.

"Well he might have been a outlaw, but I guess he was a mighty brave man," one of the men said. "Don't know as I'd have stayed around and taken on that Indian."

"He was an outlaw all right," Sheriff Buford said. "Rode with the Wild Bunch. Some folks who saw him around town say he was Tom O'Day, but he signed that ransom note Kid Curry, and that there Curry was the meanest one in the whole outfit. Who was he, young Penrose? Did he tell you his name?"

"Yes sir. He told me he was Kid Curry."

"Well then, that explains it," Buford said. "He don't look like much now, but the man was sheer terror in his day, plenty mean enough to take a hunk out of that Indian's leg."

I smiled. He'd almost missed his horse when he charged out of that bank. The Kid was a sheer terror, all right.

EIGHTEEN

The sheriff sent one of the men on ahead to the little town of Wolf. He wanted to spread the word all over the county that the Indian was dead, and that they'd found me too and I was alive. Then we started z-ing down that mountain. It was scary, but the horses didn't seem to mind, and after a while I got so that I didn't, either. It felt like we were coming down from the moon, in a way. Sheridan looked like a little toy town made out of wooden blocks on a dark green rug, but as we got closer to earth, the prairie lifted up to meet us and we couldn't see Sheridan any more.

After a while, over to one side and down below us, we could see Wolf. The Kid had said it was so small it didn't even have a bank to rob, that all it had was a school, a church, and a jail. Well, Wolf had grown since he had been there, I guessed, even though it still didn't have a bank. I could see a grocery store that had a big Coca Cola sign, and a garage where you could get gasoline.

I listened as much as I could and didn't ask questions, wondering what they thought had happened, and hoping they wouldn't arrest me for helping to rob the bank. Finally I got it figured out.

The Kid hadn't robbed the Sheridan bank at all. He'd just pretended to rob it to fool me. What he'd done was mail a ransom note to my grandmother, giving my father two weeks to come up with twenty thousand dollars! So that news hit the town like a thunderbolt. The new transatlantic cable had about got burned up with messages to my father, who was rushing back to America on a steamer.

Then a day after that, the sheriff got a tip that Arosho had been at the rodeo, and that he was hiding out in the Big Horns. Well, that was even bigger news than the kidnapping, because the Indian had the blood lust and was wanted for killing a family of picnickers. So Sheriff Buford rounded up some men to track him down. But he hadn't expected to solve both crimes at the same time. He thought I'd been taken to Denver, where it would be easier to hide me out.

I didn't know what to think about the Kid. He'd saved my life, so I couldn't hate him too much. But he'd tricked me into thinking he was Kid Curry, then tricked me into thinking he needed me to help him rob the bank. Then while I held the horses, he tricked me into thinking he was robbing it.

I stared at the lump under Grandmother's blanket, which was tied onto that big red horse. You always had to have a plan, didn't you, Kid? I asked him, in a way. Well, what was your plan, once you got the ransom money from my father? Would that have been the end of the partnership?

But I felt relieved, too. That posse wasn't bringing me in in handcuffs, and nobody knew I had meant to be a criminal. . . .

But then I also thought: Grandmother's blankets. My gosh. How am I going to explain the fact that I have all her blankets? There was other stuff too that Grandmother was sure to recognize, like about half her kitchen. How come I have all that stuff, if he was the one who kidnapped me? It gave me a lot to think about, and not much time.

There was a big crowd in Wolf, waiting for us. Some reporters had driven over from Sheridan and snapped pictures of us riding into town. Then they got the bodies off Old Red, who didn't like their smell by that time and was glad to be rid of them. They stretched them out on blankets and took pictures of Arosho and the man who had killed him, and wanted me in the same picture, but I wouldn't do it. They took plenty of pictures of me anyway, and asked me questions about my ordeal, and I had to find out what "ordeal" meant before I could answer them. More than anything, it meant when I'd been tied up and staked out like a piece of meat, and freezing to death. I told them I hadn't liked it at all.

Then the sheriff said, "All right, that's enough now, this brave boy needs to see the doctor and I'm taking him back to town." So they put me in the back seat of the sheriff's car and he and Deputy Jed and me started to drive off.

Everybody waved at me like I was special, so I waved back. I saw where some other cars had pulled up, including a big black one that was a hearse. Poor old Tom, I thought, with a lump in my throat. I kind of wished he was with me, too. Because right after we got in the car, the sheriff started asking me questions, and I needed someone with experience in being a fraud.

"Don't lie to me, boy," Sheriff Clifford Buford said to me as we drove into town. "I can spot a lie a mile off, and there's some things about your story that don't add up."

That put me in a real pickle, because I believed him. "No sir, I won't lie," I said—and I didn't, either.

When he asked me how come I'd gone with Kid Curry, I told him it was because the Kid had a gun. That was sort of the truth. But he wanted to know about the blankets and the pots and pans and the food, because he'd heard me say they belonged to my grandmother. How did Kid Curry come to have all those things that belonged to my grandmother? he asked. She'd never said anything about any of it having been stolen.

I told him how me and the Kid had been friends before he'd kidnapped me, which was the truth. I told him I'd met him one day at the monkey cage, where he lived, and I'd felt sorry for him and given him some food and Grandmother's blankets. All of that was sort of the truth, too—at least if you took it apart, instead of strung it all together.

Then I told the sheriff I hadn't expected him to kidnap me at all, which was the absolute truth. But I said I still liked the Kid even after I found out what he had done, without saying I'd only found out that day. I said I liked him because he told me stories all the time, and showed me his pistol. And I told him how the Kid had saved me from Arosho, too; how he'd snuck up to me the night it hailed, and cut me loose, and made the plan that saved my life.

The sheriff frowned, and I knew he wasn't satisfied. "It still don't sound to me like you was particularly worried about being kidnapped," he said.

"I wasn't," I said, which was the truth.

"Well, how come you wasn't?" he demanded. "Did you just figure everything would turn out all right? Of course everybody knows your daddy is a rich lawyer. Did you just figure he'd get you out of the trouble?"

"I just didn't think about it, sir," I said, which was still the truth.

"Now don't you lie to me, boy!" he suddenly thundered. "The two of you was in it together! You was going to let your daddy pay off that ransom, then split it between you!"

"Oh, no sir, I didn't know anything at all about the ransom!"

"You didn't know about the ransom? Well, now wait a minute. You knew you'd been kidnapped, didn't you?"

"Yes sir," I said, which was kind of the truth, because he didn't ask me *when* I knew I'd been kidnapped.

"Then how come you didn't know about the ransom?"

"I don't know, Sheriff. Tom—I mean, the Kid—he just never told me about any ransom." I decided the best thing to do was let the sheriff figure it out.

"Leave the boy alone, Clifford," Deputy Jed said. He'd been driving, but he'd been listening, too. "This boy ain't no criminal. Besides, why would the kidnapper tell the victim about the ransom?"

Sheriff Clifford Buford kept the frown on his face, but nodded his head. "Well, there's something that's fishy here, but I don't know what it is. I guess it don't much matter, though," he said.

Grandmother Galdbreath was glad to see me, and hugged me and cried, and told me how she'd been worried to death and had known I'd been killed, and hadn't slept for three days. She just plain was not going to ever let me out of her sight again—at least, not while I was in Sheridan. I asked her how I should go to the bathroom then. She told me I was not to make fun of her, and that I knew what she meant, and that she had a telephone call in to my dad who was worried sick about me too, even though he was in the middle of the Atlantic Ocean. It was amazing to her that we'd soon be talking to him on the telephone, she said, because she'd always thought telephones take wires, and he was on an ocean liner.

By that time I'd settled down and was feeling pretty good. I'd got by the sheriff, and knew my picture would be in tomorrow's newspaper, and it was easy for me to see that Grandmother Galdbreath really meant it when she said she was glad to see me. The funny thing was that listening to her talk reminded me of the Kid. I'd never seen her excited to where she would talk a blue streak, without caring whether any of it made sense.

Maybe that had been Tom's trouble all his life, I thought. Maybe the reason he would talk for hours at a time was some kind of excitement he had felt in his stomach.

Miss Landusky came over to visit the next day. "Well. How does it feel, having your picture in the paper and being famous?" she asked a few minutes later when we were alone.

"It feels okay." She'd brought a pie, and it really

tasted good. "This is sure good pie, Miss Landusky."

"Thank you, Alex. I made it special for you." She sat down across from me and smoothed out a wrinkle in her dress. "Do you mind if I ask you some questions?"

I did, but I couldn't tell her that. "No'm."

"Do you really think the man who kidnapped you was Kid Curry?"

How could I tell her something different from what I'd told everybody else? "I guess so. That's what he told me."

"Yes, but what was he like?" she asked. "Did he talk a blue streak? Did he say and do funny things, a bit like a clown?" She leaned forward, like she didn't want to miss a word.

"Yes'm," I said, nodding my head. "That's just the way he was."

"And he had blue eyes, about as blue as the sky?"

"Yes'm, that's him all right."

She sighed. "No, Alex, that wasn't Kid Curry. The man I've described was Tom O'Day." She leaned back in her chair. "Kid Curry's eyes were dark as clouds. And he was a quiet man who didn't waste any motion, almost the opposite of Tom. No one ever thought of Kid Curry as a clown."

I cleared my throat, trying to think what to tell her. "Well, he talked a lot, that's true, but didn't you tell me one time how people change?" I asked. "Besides, he showed me your picture."

"He did!" That made her smile. "I gave Tom my picture thirty years ago. How nice of him to have kept it."

It was just an old picture, I thought. Why was that nice?

"What really happened, Alex? Will you tell me?"

Doggone her anyway, I thought, wrestling with myself. At first I'd wanted to tell someone all about it, but the farther away it got, the less I wanted to tell the whole story. "He kidnapped me," I said. "That's all."

"You mean he held a gun to your head and forced you to go with him or he'd shoot you?"

The pie got less and less interesting. "No'm, he didn't have to do all that."

"Well, what did he do?"

I didn't say anything. I couldn't.

"You don't have to tell me if you don't want to, Alex, but I hope you'll tell me some of it. You see, I knew Tom as well as anyone, and I knew Arosho, too. And I loved both of them. It just seems so awful that they should kill one another."

"You loved Arosho?" I asked.

"Oh yes. He was such a proud and fine young man."

"He was a killer, Miss Landusky. He was gonna kill me!"

"Please tell me about Arosho, Alex?" she asked.

So I told her. I wanted to tell her, too, because there were some things about him I couldn't get out of my mind. I started with how the Kid and I knew something funny was going on when someone put rocks in his boots. Then how the plan to catch Arosho misfired and I got caught instead, and Arosho tied me up like bait and waited. But the Kid cut me loose, and the next day, he shot Arosho after Arosho'd stabbed him. I even told her how Arosho made the same sign to me he'd made to her at the parade.

She listened real hard and didn't interrupt, but her eyes got wet. "What a pity," she said, when I was done. "Two brave men." Her hands kind of fluttered, and her head rocked back and forth. "The sign Arosho gave you. Would you show me?"

I stood up and put one hand by my stomach, palm down. Then I moved my hand away kind of slow, keeping it flat with the ground.

"He could have killed you then, Alex."

"He could?"

"Yes. He had some strength left, didn't he? And he had that knife in his hand, or he could have picked up Tom's gun."

"Golly." I hadn't thought of that. "Why didn't he?"

"Perhaps out of respect."

"Me?" I asked. "I'm only twelve years old. Why would he respect me?"

"I don't know." She looked at me and smiled. "Perhaps he knows you better than you know yourself."

That made me feel strange.

"Do you know what the sign means?" she asked.

"No'm."

"It means 'Your world, not mine. I will not live in it.'"

"Why would he want to tell me that?"

"Their world—his world—has changed so much, and so quickly! Not long ago—and possibly forever, before that—the town of Sheridan and the land all around for hundreds of miles was the hunting ground for the Crow. Now most of the animals are gone."

"Well, that's sad and all," I said. "But does it mean he should go around killing families and old men?"

"No, of course not. But to Arosho and his people, *all* life is important, not just human lives. According to their view, the two-legged creatures have no more right to the earth than the four-legged ones." Her sad eyes kind of drifted behind me somewhere. "You have no idea of the slaughter of animals that occurred right here in Sheridan," she said. "Thousands upon thousands—possibly even millions—of buffalo were senselessly destroyed. Even I can remember when the prairies were filled with herds of elk and antelope, and packs of coyotes and wolves. Now they are gone."

For a minute I was back up in the Big Horns, z-ing off the mountain toward Wolf. I looked down and saw the prairie, green and full of animals, maybe the way it used to look. "Huh."

She smiled at me but didn't really see me. I wondered

if she could see it, too. "All he wanted was to save the earth from the ravages of the whites."

"Huh," I said again, wondering for a minute what was right, and what was wrong. Then I was back in my grandmother's living room. "I wish he hadn't killed Tom."

"Yes, funny old Tom, the court jester," she said, still smiling. "I thought I knew him. But he stayed up there and waited for a chance to save your life, when every impulse in his body must have told him to run! To go get the money!"

"He had to save me, Miss Landusky," I said. "Without me he never would have got the ransom."

"Why do you say that?"

"That's what the sheriff said. Sheriff Buford told me that."

"That simply isn't true, Alex. The bank had been instructed to pay the money to Tom on demand, no questions asked."

"You mean he didn't have to hand me over to get the money?"

"That's right, young man. That's the way you do business with kidnappers."

"I don't get it. They'd have given him the money even if I was dead?"

"Yes. Incredible, isn't it?" She smiled, kind of wondering about it. "No one would have known you were dead—not until someone found your body. So he could have gotten away with it. He finally produced a scheme that would have worked."

"Gosh." I hadn't even eaten the crust, which was the best part. "Why did he do it then?"

"I don't know. He must have loved you, Alex." That made me feel really strange, to think an old man like that could have loved me! "And—perhaps—you gave him more than he gave you."

"I didn't give him anything," I said. I had to talk real carefully because of the lump in my throat.

"Oh yes, you did," she said, smiling at me the way my real mother used to smile. "You gave him what he wanted more than anything—even more than his own life. You gave him courage."

"Huh!" I said again. Maybe we'd been partners after all.

She started to get up. It took a while, and I could hear a lot of popping in her joints. "You know, Alex, your father is a very good lawyer," she said, when she was on her feet.

"Yes'm, I know."

"What are you going to tell him? Simply that you were kidnapped, and went along with Tom because he had a gun?"

"Well, that's what happened, Miss Landusky," I said. "Sort of."

She nodded, like she didn't really believe me. "I have the feeling you're leaving out some of the detail. Do you think you can survive a cross-examination by your father, without providing him with the details?"

My dad and step-mom were downstairs, talking to Grandmother Galdbreath, after driving up from Denver in that old Packard. After all the hugs and handshakes and kisses and all that mushy stuff was out of the way, I'd gone up to my room to pack my suitcase.

I sure felt different about a lot of things. I'd been real glad to see them, but even that was different, like I was older. I lifted a corner of the rug and picked up that old wanted poster Miss Landusky had given me. I stared at it a minute, then stuck it in the bottom of my suitcase, under the clean shirts Grandmother had washed and ironed.

You old fraud, I thought to myself, smiling as I thought about Tom O'Day. You saved my life, when you could have run off with twenty thousand dollars in your pocket.

Then I looked out the window, across the street, at the house that sat there and the yard around it. For a minute I was in a grove of cottonwood trees, watching a deer who was watching me.

"Hurry up, Alex!" my dad yelled, from downstairs. "We don't have all day!"

I wasn't real anxious to start the ride back to Denver with my dad. He'd want to know all about everything that had happened, including the kidnapping. But I wasn't going to tell him any more than I'd already told the sheriff. I might get a licking, but a licking—even a good one—wouldn't last for more than a day or two.

Maybe that's what's different, I thought. For a whole summer, I'd been a cowboy named "Cloudy," who hooked up with Kid Curry, the famous outlaw. Together, we'd robbed the Sheridan bank. The way I felt, it was my story, not my dad's.

Maybe some day, I'd feel like telling him about it. But until I wanted to, it was strictly between my partner and me.